WITHDRAWN

A Diplomat's Daughter

written by
Victoria Montes

photographs and illustratons by
Janie K. Gilbert

BOUNCING BALL BOOKS
"From the Florida Swamp to Readers Everywhere"

A Diplomat's Daughter

written by Victoria Montes
photographs and illustrations by Janie K. Gilbert

This novel is a work of fiction. Any references to real events, businesses, organizations, and locales are intended only to give the fiction a sense of reality and authencity. Any resemblence to actual persons, living or dead, is entirely coincidental.

Copyright Library of Congress © 2007 by Victoria Montes
All rights Reserved

Registration Library of Congress
ISBN 13 978-1-934138-14-4
ISBN 10 1-934138-14-2
EAN 9-781934-138144

Printed in Jerusalem, Israel 2007

dr.ball
www.bouncingballbooks.com

Acknowledgement

I'd like to thank my family for their help with this book; my father, Alvin Gilbert, a United States diplomat, who passed away the summer of 2006 before the book was released, my mother Janie Gilbert, an artist and photographer, who did the artwork on location during the experience, my siblings Annslie, Tom, Brett, and Tony who shared many of my experiences, and my sons Thomas and Tony who put up with me during my writing.

Dedication

The diplomatic community of the United States of America made me part of their family.

I especially trusted the Marines assigned to the American Embassy in Islamabad in 1979 who made me feel like nothing bad could happen to us, not on their watch.

Steven Crowley gave his life for that promise.

Forward

A Diplomat's Daughter is based on a true story and accurately depicts Islamic culture at the places and times in the novel. Historical events are written according to the experiences I had when I was in Pakistan. The novel takes the reader to Islamabad from 1978 through 1979 and covers the invasion of Afghanistan by the Soviet Union, the hanging of Prime Minister Bhutto, and the attack on the American Embassy. I have first hand knowledge of these events because I was a diplomat's daughter there until 1979.

These were tense times for the United States and Iran; Iranian students stormed the American Embassy and took hostages. The repercussions of this event were felt in Islamabad; crowds stormed the American Embassy, leaving sixty diplomats trapped in a burning building and a nineteen year-old Marine fatally shot. Amidst this turmoil, the protagonist, Ronni Wasp, longs to matter to people, fit in, and belong in her world as a diplomat's daughter.

My father, Alvin Gilbert, a United States diplomat, passed away the summer of 2006 before the book was released. My mother, Janie Gilbert, is an artist and photographer and did artwork on location during the experience.

Chapter One

"Would you get your knob of an elbow away from me?" Shifting, I attempted to dislodge the tip of my younger sister's elbow from my side. "The bony thing's bruising my ribs." The seats of the plane were close together, and she'd crossed into my space as she tried to peer over my shoulder at my *Seventeen* magazine.

Her annoying echo came back, "The bony thing's bruising my ribs."

"Shut up! God, you're irritating."

"Shut up! God, you're irritating," she imitated me.

"My name's Amy, and I'm an idiot," I said, hoping Amy'd parrot me and call herself a fool.

"My name's Ronni, and I'm an idiot."

Steaming, I looked out the small round window. *Adopted—switched in the hospital. No way I was related to Amy, the lame brain.* We didn't even look alike. I had dishwater blonde hair with green eyes while she had black hair and brown eyes. Besides, as my younger sister by a year and a half, she was taller and a stick figure, while I had what my boyfriend Shawn called a pinchable butt. *Shawn, why couldn't my parents have left me with you and your family?* I had planned my whole summer. My best friend Valeria and I planned on swimming across the Strait of Gibraltar from Morocco to Spain. I was supposed to graduate with my friends. One day I'd marry Shawn. This move messed up my life.

The pilot announced our arrival first in English, then in Arabic. Below us lay a patchwork of asphalt. We were supposed to land on that thing? I received another stab to the ribs.

"If you don't cut it out, this magazine is going to collide with your big nose."

"Mom," Amy called. "Ronni threatened to punch me in the nose."

"Ronni, just quit," Mom said from her seat directly in front of us. She sat next to my dad.

What kind of hell was Dad getting us into this time? We were supposed to stay in Morocco for three more years. I was supposed to be with Shawn—attend the spring dance. I met Shawn my freshman year of high school almost a year before, when he'd been my lab partner in Biology. I loved the way his blonde curls brushed against his light eyelashes just over baby blue eyes, and the way he smiled lopsided with only the left side of his lip curling upward. He was as cute as Christopher Atkins in the *Blue Lagoon.* But, something happened, and we'd cut our tour short and left for some country called Pakistan.

As a diplomat and an agriculture attaché, Dad traveled to countries for two to four years. These were called tours and they usually started at the beginning of a new school year, but not this trip. It was April and we had been uprooted to leave without much explanation two months before my freshman year ended.

My father tried to make it sound exciting, "Interestingly enough, it used to be India and was split up in the time of Gandhi. India and Pakistan have been enemies ever since." Big deal. All I knew about India was children were starving, and if I didn't shut up and eat, my mom would send my food there.

Mom peered into her compact as she used the teasing comb to coax stray strands of short dark hair into place. She finished, checked her eyeliner, and picked up the sketching pad on which she had drawn a perfect copy of my father's hand. Thank God, I sat behind her and not beside her as an enlisted model. "Ronni, stop twitching, tip your head to the right, no, don't move!" How many hours had I heard those phrases when she had captured me for that cruel and unusual punishment? I think she loved art more than anything else in the world. Dad, Amy, and I had been dragged through museums all over the world.

My father sat directly in front of me. He blended into the background as if he were a piece of PIA, Pakistan International Airlines. I'd never heard of PIA. Dad didn't care. He had the *New York Tribune*, the *Washington Post,* and the *Auburn Gazette.* He worked all of the crossword puzzles. If we crashed, would the fire department find him the sole survivor calmly finishing three down?

The wheels banged against the ground, thrusting me forward, then back. Through ears clogged from changing altitude, I heard the tires go "flup, flup, flup" as they bounced. The plane shuddered so violently I feared it would shatter into a thousand pieces. It would explode into a huge fireball and I would never see Shawn again.

When it stopped, the door opened and a blast of angry air greeted us. There was no tunnel leading to the airport. No, in this country we stumbled down the stairs and walked to the airport. The air pressed against my face like a hot, sweaty towel. The blazing sun stabbed my eyeballs. I moved along behind my parents, an ant in a procession.

My dad started blabbing, "You'll be interested to know that Islamabad, the capital of Pakistan, means home of Islam in Urdu, the official language here." He turned around to me with a stupid grin. I didn't care if it meant home of John Travolta, Donny Osmond, and Shawn Cassidy. It wasn't my home, and it never would be.

We entered a large room lit only by sunlight blasting through the windows. White spots, where the sun had eaten away at my vision, danced before me. Foul foot odor penetrated the building. The terminal wasn't huge like Kennedy or Dulles, the airports we flew into every two years when we went on home leave—when we got to go back to the States for summer vacation and pig out on McDonalds and Lucky Charms cereal.

We passed through customs but no one inspected my purse or the two carry-on bags that hung heavily from each of my shoulders. Then we moved on to the baggage area, guarded by sweaty men armed with rifles. They wore wrinkled uniforms the color of butcher paper. Hoping they wouldn't point a gun at me, I avoided looking at them.

Our luggage arrived, and next to my suitcase stood the dog carrier, holding our four-year-old German shepherd, Juma Maguardi. Her name meant "Friday Night Watch" in Arabic. We got her on our tour in Nigeria.

She yelped as she saw us, and I ran to her. "Hi, Juma, girl." My fingers reached for her through the bars.

Juma got her name because one Friday night we were robbed. Our night watchman fell asleep on the job. Dad found us a real "Juma Maguardi" instead, and we were never robbed again.

One of the airport security guards edged towards the cage, bending his knees, and stooping to peer inside, his rifle held in front of him as a shield. Juma let out a low growl, and the guard sprang back fingering the trigger.

"No, girl." I clicked my tongue to calm her, fearing the guard might decide to shoot her. "It's okay." My eyes stayed on the trigger of the guard's rifle.

Juma tried to stand, but the cage was too short and her tail thumped rapidly against the bars. A rumble hummed from her chest and became a high-pitched whine for freedom. I recognized the cry as the same one rising in my chest.

"Sorry, girl, you'll be okay."

"Very sorry," my dad said to the guard, who stepped aside with a grunt. Dad had commandeered a cart from somewhere—its owner stood next to it with a terrified look. Dad hesitated a moment, then said, "Okay, gang let's get this cage on the cart." Juma ducked, whined, and paced as we lifted the crate, which must have weighed two hundred pounds.

Dad began steering the cart towards the exit, and I adjusted my carry-on bags again before hurrying to follow my family.

We headed toward the front of the airport. A sea of faces pressed against the glass walls separating us from the outside. Their eyes bored through me, palms streaked the glass, mouths called words that were only a mumble through the pane. This mob could smoother us. *What if they attacked? They could probably eat for a month on what our stuff was worth. And the police, what would they care if another greedy American was killed?*

We reached the door and moved through those dark people, foreign people, blind people, crippled people, dirty people. Dad led the way, pushing the cart. Amy walked in front of Mom and I stepped behind Mom as though she'd protect me with her sketch pad and hairspray. Avoiding eye contact, I pretended not to notice the scary people with twisted limbs and fly-caked eyes. *Please God, let me get through this crowd without dying.*

The crowd of mostly men pushed in on us. They wore pajama-like clothes, which might have been white at one time. An odor of curry perfumed their stale sweat, so thick I could taste it.

A man wearing a Harvard sweatshirt pushed me. Mom moved ahead of Amy. As I stumbled against my sister, I spotted a man sporting a filthy Boston Red Socks t-shirt—perhaps stolen from his last victim, a baseball fan who ventured into the crowd only to end up dead. Hands grabbed at my dress, but I twisted out of their grip. I couldn't go back into the airport so I pushed forward. *Get away from me.*

"Memsahib, I help you," came from every direction. The crowd surged around me like a human sea; grasping fingers snatched my carry-on.

"No! Stop!" I tried to tug back, but my bag disappeared. "Help, they're stealing my stuff."

Other cracked palms held out strange silver coins begging me to add to the amount, but they weren't getting the rest of my gear. Clutching the two remaining bags, I stood ready for a fight.

"Hey, those are our suitcases," I heard Mom's voice from up ahead. "Wait, James, they're taking our bags." Juma began to bark and I looked at the cart where a boy dropped a bag and ran away. I chose the wrong family member to walk with. Juma, the night watch, was also a good suitcase protector.

I soon lost sight of her again as voices and bodies came from everywhere, "I help you, only two rupees."

"One rupee, memsahib. No worries."

My sweaty, blue, summer dress clung to my skin like plastic wrap. A pair of gnarled hands shoved a squalling baby into my face. A rash mottled its cheeks; its eyes were bright with fever. I squeezed against the building and pushed in between Amy and Mom who were taller than me so I could block the people from my view. Even when I concentrated on my mom's shoes, which created a small dust cloud as they struck the blackened walkway, I couldn't block out the sandaled feet powdered with dust.

"James, are you keeping an eye on the luggage?" Mom's tearful voice rose above the relentless begging. "They've taken everything. Do we even have a car?" Shoot. What if he forgot to arrange for a car? We couldn't walk all the way with the crowd grabbing at us.

Suddenly, Mom came to a halt, and I peeked around her to see a man as tall as Dad and dark as wheat toast striding towards us. His coarse hair and beard of midnight black contrasted sharply with his flowing shirt, as white as sugar. He raised a piece of gray cardboard lettered with red ink: "Wasp," it read. He stopped in front of my father. "You being sahib Bass?"

Dad nodded. "Yes, I'm James Wasp."

"My name is Ahmed. The car being dis way." He pointed off in the distance and led us through the crowd. To my amazement, the beggars parted before him.

As we reached a white Jeep, a parade of men piled our bags up next to it. Juma kept twirling around in the cage barking at anyone who ventured too close. The bag snatchers hovered around my dad. "Only five rupees, sahib."

"Three rupees, memsahib. I three bags." They'd grabbed my bag and wanted money for bringing it back. What kind of racket was that?

The men argued in some strange dialect. "Ach'haa-ach'ha."

Ahmed gave the suitcase bandits little silver-colored coins picturing Queen Elizabeth of England. I climbed into the refreshing environment of the air-conditioned Jeep. As Ahmed swung into the driver's seat, the men who had been paid surged around us. Smiling and nodding, they lightly tapped on the window glass. Then they called out happily as our Jeep picked its way out of the parking lot.

We emerged onto a dirt highway where traffic traveled in all directions in the same lanes. I clawed at the vinyl seat trying to hold the Jeep back from at least a dozen near misses. The driver used the horn to herd an old man on a bike with no tires. The man turned, shouted, and raised his fist, almost colliding with the donkey cart before him. I turned to watch him continue to pedal away on bent rims.

Tin houses with corrugated roofs lined the sides of the road. The front of one home was a large piece of tin with a cut-out door. Another house had tires and metal parts rusting out front—people sat on them watching us drive by. Two women, covered from head to toe in tent-like dresses, walked by scrawny dogs searching for food in the puddles. In Morocco, the women didn't wear those tents. Some even wore jeans. I had arrived in a country that didn't like anyone of my gender and wasn't that reason enough to get out right away? Chickens flapped and fluttered across the street to avoid bikes and carts. We'd arrived in hell.

The Jeep made a smooth right turn onto a paved road. Beyond an iron gate, a brick and concrete three-story building stood in front of a grassy circle with a large pole in the center. The American flag lay motionless against the pole, like a dog beaten down by the still heat. Hurray, the Embassy, finally—friendly American soil. The gate guard waved us through. The black iron gate fencing off the area made sure poverty stayed outside.

We drove by the embassy and down the hill, stopping in front of a building with a sign posted, "American Club House." Beside it loomed apartment complexes. Ahmed turned to Dad and said, "Dis being it, sahib. You stay here. Da house not being ready."

Dad looked back at us and ordered, "Ronni, let Juma out to get a drink and walk around. Everyone grab a bag. Let's go."

We took what we could and headed down the steps toward one of the large, brick, three-story, condo-like buildings. I put Juma on a leash and she pulled me down the stairs and ran across the jaundiced-looking grass in the center of three blocks of buildings, dragging me behind her. I yanked and steered her toward a few benches while I readjusted my carry-on. Juma stopped at two leafless shrubs and sniffed their trunks. Suddenly, she lifted her head and bolted around the monkey bars, swing set, and jungle gym before dashing back to Mom and Amy. Sweat beaded on my forehead. It must have been one hundred degrees. Juma jumped on Mom.

"Hold her!" Mom brushed imaginary paw prints from her crisp linen suit. *You try to hold her*, I thought but didn't say anything. "Just tie her to the railing here and we'll get her water later," Mom added. I took Juma over to the stairs leading up to the complex number three, which Dad climbed. I quickly tied her leash and left her to whine and bark after us.

Dad stopped one flight of stairs up and in front of door number twelve. The door swung open before my dad's fist struck it.

In the opened doorframe, a tall, wide-smiling woman stood. "Well, hello. I'm Doris Calloway." She swung one arm wide, almost hitting the shorter woman standing behind her. "Come on in. We got the unit all fixed up for y'all's arrival."

The shorter woman with honey complexion and dark hair cut in a short pageboy waved at us. "Hi I'm Maria O'Malley," one of your sponsors. I have some lemonade in the refrigerator. Come in, come in." Sponsors were people who showed you around.

Mom and Dad walked in, leaving Amy and me in the doorway, directly in front of Doris Calloway. In her high heels, Doris stood six feet tall, eyelevel with Amy and taller than me.

"Hi, girls. Welcome. You're gonna love it here." She hugged us to her amble bosom smashing me against Amy. I had to fight for my breath and avoid pulling away from the overly friendly woman. She let us go. "Everyone is just dying ta meet ya. Come on in and put down them big, heavy bags."

I looked over at Amy and crossed my eyes. Amy bit her lip as if stifling a laugh.

The furniture was beige and matched—like motel room decor. I headed for the chair on the farthest end of the living room to get out of the way of the adults in case anyone decided to hug me again.

What I really wanted to do was find the shower, change into shorts, and turn on The Movie Channel. But this room had no television, a clear indication there were no movies, or even television shows like, *Happy Days* or *Fantasy Island*.

Sinking into the burlap-textured chair, I searched through my carry-on for the *Seventeen* magazine.

"Here you are, dear." Mrs. Calloway stood in front of me holding a blue stuffed rabbit. Just beyond, Amy held a white rabbit. *Could this day get any weirder?* Amy lifted hers up and did a little dance with it behind Mrs. Calloway's back.

Mrs. Calloway shoved the toy into my hand. I forced a smile. Juma could always use another chew toy.

I got up. "I'm going to give Juma water." Dad filled a bowl with water and handed it to me. In the courtyard, I sat beside her running my hand through her fur as she lapped water into my lap. I wanted to scream, "Let me out of here. I want to go home!" *What was Shawn doing?* I took out the half silver heart around my neck, the one Shawn gave me when he swore he'd always love me. *He'll rescue me,* I thought as tears sprang to my eyes. *I'd go back and stay with his family. They'd be glad to have me.* I polished the jagged heart with the hem of my dress and visualized the two of us next to his pool surrounded by friends laughing about my brief torturous stay in Pakistan.

When I dried my eyes and got back to the apartment, I lugged my suitcase into the room. I unsnapped my bag and my diary slid out. I picked it up and held it to my chest. *My memories—my whole life on paper.* I opened it and found the twenty and four ones I had hidden there. *My traveling money.* I would save every cent I earned and get back to Morocco—back to Shawn and my other friends.

I put the diary on the nightstand and reached into the bag to retrieve my jewelry box. Mom had one made for each of us. Our names were brass inlay in Arabic script. Arabic characters curl and flow, more like a design than letters of an alphabet. I ran my hand across the dark polished wood, then opened the lid and took out a long strand of ivory pukka shells. We had spent our Christmas holiday on Bali with Shawn and his family.

Shawn bought me the shells, but I never wore them. They covered up my half heart.

Shawn and his family had stayed with us in grass huts right off the beach. When the winds blew, we were afraid we'd be bombarded with coconuts from surrounding trees.

At night, everyone met in the large open grass hut that served as the dining room. For dessert we ate "Big Mama's" rice pudding. Big Mama was the large muumuu-wearing hut owner.

After dinner, our families had walked the streets together. One night, Shawn and I strolled ahead and three young, bronze women with off-the-shoulder, short, flowered dresses beckoned shamelessly to him. He strode toward one with black hair tumbling across her shoulders. Then he stopped and pointed at me, "No, my wife won't let me."

"Oh yeah, where is she?" I teased him. When he hugged me, I knew we fit. I had to get back to him, to Morocco. And as soon as I saved enough money, I would.

Chapter Two

The next morning, a banging on our door announced our sponsors—the O'Malley's, an embassy family assigned to show us around. There were two O'Malley sisters. Both were short and dark with noses that looked like they'd been broken in a fight and thick eyebrows that looked like mini rain-clouds over their brown eyes. Nancy was sixteen, a year older than I. The second daughter, Susan, was in Amy's class.

They breezed into the living room with a basket of plums, dates, and mangos. Amy plucked one out of the basket and brought it to her mouth, but I hesitated. "They're safe to eat. We soaked them in bleach," Mrs. O'Malley assured me. "Would you like to join us for a fish fry on the Indus River? There'll be other American families," she continued. *Maybe, I'd make a friend before I had to start school.*

"We drive over the Indus River," Susan added with a smile.

Drive? Wouldn't we need a boat to get across the mighty Indus River?

The night before Dad had droned on about how the Indus stretched the length of the entire country. Melting snow from the Himalayan Mountains, in the north of Pakistan, fed the river and it emptied into the warm Arabian Sea in the south.

It was okay with my parents, so we packed into two white Jeeps, our driver following the O'Malley's, and took off for the Indus. The road was pockmarked and narrow and we drove in a dust cloud kicked up by the

O'Malley's Jeep. Though dull in comparison, it made the one from the airport seem like a superhighway. We rocked and swayed as Ahmed swerved to miss holes along the way, throwing Amy up against me.

"I think I'm getting car sick," Amy complained.

"Just don't throw up on me," I yelled and pushed her away.

"Oh, look at the mustard plants," My mom said. "They'd be great in a portrait." I looked out the window as the tiny buds the color of dandelions rushed by on both sides of the streets.

We reached a ribbon of water over which wooden planks lay. Ahmed, our driver, stopped the Jeep and announced, "Dis being it, sahib."

This little stream two vehicles wide was the Indus River? While I stared in amazement, the Jeep entered the clear rushing waters. As the current lapped up towards the doors, I peered out my window and asked, "What if the car doesn't make it through?" Would we get stuck and have to wade through the water and walk all the way home?

"De oxen." Ahmed pointed to a pair of white horned beasts with large wet nostrils standing at the water's edge.

The engine coughed, and I held my breath. The water probably hid water snakes and leeches. The wheels sank into the boards as they bent with the weight, but we rolled on. When we emerged on the other side, everyone let out a collective nervous laugh. "Let's do that again," Amy said.

The engine sputtered until we picked up speed, and we followed the shore as the river widened and the bank rose a few feet above it. Up ahead I saw tents with campfires lit in front of them. On the fires sat huge brass, flat-bottomed pans overflowing with what might have been rice. Farther up, bare-chested men threw white nets out into the water.

A cluster of American kids ranging from first graders to high school seniors huddled together waiting to board one of two camels. Nancy led us over to the group. "Guys, this is Ronni and Amy. They're new."

A tight ring of almost a half a dozen strangers, who looked closest to my age, opened up. I smiled and waved. In the middle a redheaded, freckled guy nodded as he extended a hand holding a lighter. "Oh." He shifted the Bic to his other hand and shook mine. "Name's Ian." His broad smile revealed slightly crooked front teeth, which reminded me to keep my mouth shut over my own hideous braces. The girl closest to Ian smiled tightly and said, "Jennifer, nice to meet you." She brushed a strand of black hair behind her ear and leaned in to ignite her cigarette with Ian's lighter.

A blonde girl on the other side of Ian gave me a quick nod, readjusted her glasses and said, "Hi, Susan and . . ." she tapped a short ebony-skinned girl beside her. "Mary."

Mary smiled, looked away and said, "Yeah, I know what you mean. My cousin asked if I ride a camel to school."

Ian fixed his penetrating stare on me, and the brunette who called herself Jennifer took the cig from her red-lipsticked mouth and shoved his shoulder. "Hey, light my stick."

Ian flipped the Bic without moving his eyes from me. "They ask me if I smoke Camels."

Jennifer took a drag on the smoke, blew out a ring and smiled. "And if we live in huts over here."

Another brown-haired, baby-faced boy said, "I eat Camel burgers." Then he slapped his hands on the sides of his face and some brown mush shot from his mouth. It landed on the sandaled foot of a tanned girl in pigtails.

"Damn you, Danny!" she roared.

Ian blinked his left eye at me and then broke off his gaze to grab the girl with the pig-tails around the waist of her overalls. He swung her around and the other girls circled him, poking and tickling.

Had he winked at me? Ian couldn't hold a candle to Shawn in the cute department and Shawn wouldn't have so many girls around him. *Would he?*

The circle closed up again with me on the outside and Danny jumped on top of the group.

As Ian prepared to mount the camel, he turned to me and said, "Hey, Ronni, you want to get on before me?" *Why me? Did his eyes linger on me too long or was it my imagination?* Jennifer fixed her dark stare on me and flashed a plastic smile. Then she wrapped her arms around Ian as if to say, "he's mine." I grinned back at him and approached the beast.

It watched me through long, thick, dark eyelashes. As though deep in thought, it gnawed on grass through a knitted mesh-like muzzle on its mouth. Then it spat at me, green slimy spit that made me jump back. The spit hit my white converse tennis shoes. *Gross.*

The camel had two humps with a saddle balanced between them. The beast folded its long legs under its body as its handler pulled on a lead. I straddled the blanket and saddle. Ian shrugged the brunette girl off his arm and stepped next to me, holding out the reins. He brushed my hand as he placed the rough rope in my palm, and winked. I felt an uncertain tickling in my stomach. *Did this guy like me?* I nervously brushed my shoulder-length hair behind one ear. *What was I thinking? I had Shawn. I didn't need anyone else.*

The handler made a clicking sound with his tongue, and I gripped the rope. Suddenly, the camel lunged forward and then lurched back; rocking so quickly I would have been catapulted off if I hadn't tightened my grip. A startled scream escaped my lips. The group below laughed. Ian called, "You okay?" My cheeks got hot.

We made two wide circles, bobbing up and down with each step before returning. The handler clicked his tongue and the camel folded its legs, throwing me back and forth again. Feeling stupid, I stumbled off the beast and fled to the water's edge. *Was it some sort of joke? Like sending the new person to the roof of the school to look for an imaginary swimming pool. Was Ian pretending to be nice to me while setting me up to be the laughing stock?*

I held my silver half heart in my hand, and let its edge cut into my fingers. *What if I dropped it into the water and it floated south, down the Indus to the Arabian Sea? It would travel around the whole continent of Africa to Morocco and Shawn. Shawn . . .* "Hey, what you doing?" Ian's voice startled me. "Don't let the stupid camel get you down." I spun around to face him as he moved closer so that his warm arm brushed mine. His gaze shifted to my necklace, and I took my fingers away from it. Maybe Ian thought I was cute. I felt excited and then guilty about Shawn. "Where you from?" Ian asked.

"Morocco."

"Is that from your guy?" He pointed at the half-heart.

"Yeah."

"Lucky him."

What did he mean by that? Before I could find out, Ian's girlfriend rushed towards us and draped herself around him, giving me a poisonous glare. He winked and let her pull him away.

A bell chimed and I turned around to see people lining up in front of the rice pans. I returned to find plates overflowing with rice covered with dates, raisins, chili, and peppers. I stood in line behind my Dad.

The tangy fish burnt my mouth, making my lips sting for half an hour. The rice scorched my mouth, too. After searing my taste buds, I wondered if I'd ever be able to taste anything again. I fanned my burning tongue with a flat piece of pita bread.

"This is the best fish I've ever eaten. I have to get this recipe," Mom announced from her seat across from me. "Ronni, don't eat with your tongue sticking out."

I closed my mouth, ducked my head, and glanced around at what seemed like a million eyes staring at me. Amy smirked at me from her seat beside Nancy O'Malley. I didn't dare look in Ian's direction. Before the sting of Mom's comment had subsided, she left to sketch the fishermen. My mom, Mrs. Perfect, the stepdaughter of a drunk, who learned to say, "yellow" instead of "yeller" was the proper sharpened pastel and I was the embarrassing shavings.

Well, Mom wouldn't have to put up with me much longer.

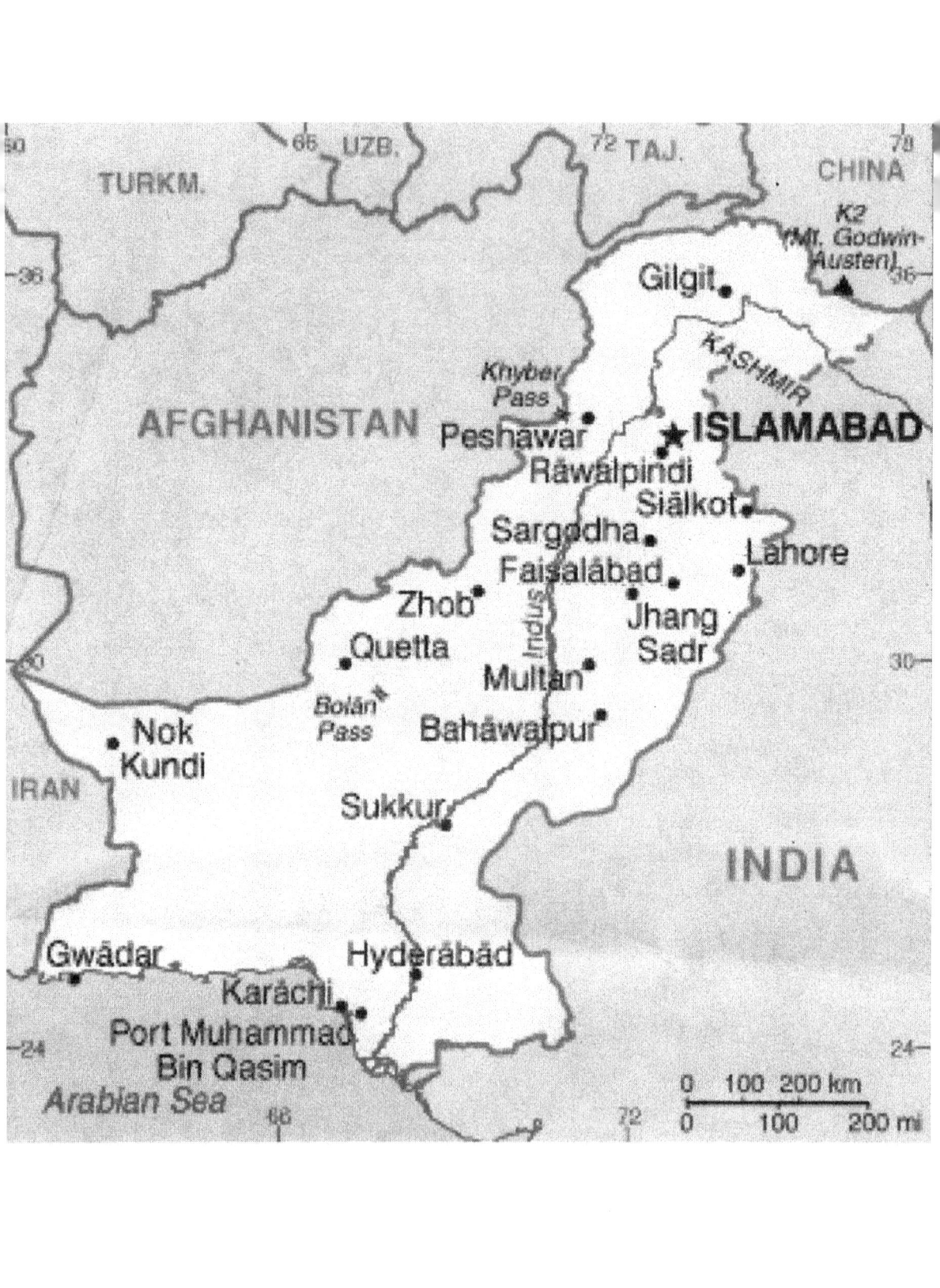

Chapter Three

As Dad climbed into the front seat of the Jeep, he turned to us and said, "You're in for a very interesting treat." Then he turned to Ahmed. "Take us to Shaharah-e-Islamabad." *What's that?* I thought. The only treat I wanted was to go back to Morocco.

We bumped along over the usual narrow, pitted roadways, when in one of the fields we spotted young girls in bright yellow, red, and blue dresses, making mud pies. "What a beautiful picture," Mom cooed, as she fumbled in her bag. "Ahmed, pull over. I want to get a photo." Ahmed looked at my father, who repeated my mother's request.

Ahmed pulled the car to a stop while Mom fiddled with her camera. We watched the girls, who were around six or seven, scoop and pat earth into round balls. They slapped the mud balls against the sides of their house.

"What are they doing? Fixing the hut?" I asked.

"How interesting. They're making cow pies with the cow manure," Dad said. "They use the compost as fuel. After it dries, it slides off the wall and they can burn it to cook their food."

"Gross." I gagged. "Doesn't the food taste like poop? Why don't they just use wood?"

"Do you see any trees?" Dad asked.

I looked around and saw only small scrawny bushes. "What about the forest?"

"Deforestation—too many trees have been cut down. That makes it hard to find wood. Manure's an alternative fuel source," Dad answered. Mom took more pictures. If we weren't careful she'd be asking for the recipe for food cooked over cow dung because she always wanted to try anything foreign.

Ten minutes later, the countryside opened up into a two-lane road with median strips of blossoming bushes, fluorescent lights, and dome-shaped buildings. "How interesting. Look." Dad pointed to the looming mountains in the background. "The Margalla Hills." In the distance they were just beautiful shades of green and purple, which set off the glimmering white mosque in the foreground. The sharp points of steeples surrounded the pointed roof of the building. *Wow!* In a matter of minutes we went from a dirt village to an industrial city with white plastered buildings and billboards of loopy black writing and pictures.

"You'll be interested to know that the Shah Faisal Mosque is still under construction," Dad said pointing to the mosque. "It was built in honor of King Faisal of Saudi Arabia. They're adding a mausoleum for General Zia, the current head of the state of Pakistan." Mom had dragged us to every museum, cathedral, and castle in the world. All I wanted to do was get home and finish my novel, *The Thorn Birds,* and listen to my new album, *Saturday Night Fever.*

The sun glistened off the four slender pencil-like steeples surrounding the main building; light filtered through the interior of the mosque and played across the great white fountain made of many triangular-shaped pieces of marble. As I gazed into the clear water, a little native boy approached us. He wore a tattered dirty shirt over equally dirty off-white shorts. "You, America?" he asked in a heavy accent.

My parents ignored him and Ahmed waved him away, but the boy ducked him, circled the fountain and approached me from the opposite side. "I can show you," he said.

What was he going to show me? "No, it's okay," I replied, backing away, while staring into his large, black eyes. He was a cute kid but his neck was rimmed with soil and dirt caked his nails.

"What you name?" he asked.

"Ronni." I watched the rest of my family move away from the fountain without waiting for me.

"Runny?"

I smiled. "No, Veronica."

"Bare Runny Ka," he pronounced.

"Runny's fine," I conceded, picturing a naked nose with snot running down it.

"Mayra naam, Rashid hay," he said pointing to himself. I didn't respond and he pounded his thin bony chest. "Rashid. Mayra naam, Rashid hay." *Oh, he was telling me his name.*

"You're Rashid?" I asked, trying out the name.

"Yes," he replied, breaking into a wide grin.

Mom and Amy walked back toward the fountain and Mom called, "Ronni, come on. Leave the boy alone unless you want to pay him for his time."

"Gotta go," I said, and hustled off after my parents.

Rashid fell back a few paces, but continued to tag along.

He was so quiet that I had almost forgotten him until we hurried toward the car to leave. Spinning my head around, I realized that he had vanished.

Dad told Ahmed to take a side road on the way home. "But sahib, dat is not being da way," Ahmed argued.

"James, not one of your shortcuts?" Mom moaned.

My dad smiled his dumb animated grin. "Let's see where this turn leads us. It's bound to be an interesting ride."

My straight-laced dad never seemed excited unless he was taking one of his short cuts. We hadn't taken one since Morocco when we took a wrong turn down a small dark street. Our headlights had picked up the figures of two men. One kicked another and the kicked man had stumbled and fallen on the hood of our car. Blood streamed down the injured man's face as he stared blankly into our windshield. Then he stumbled back towards his attacker for more punishment.

After a moment, Dad had reversed the car and we had escaped, but sometimes at night those man's blank eyes visited my dreams. We never called the police because we didn't understand the situation in a foreign country. We never mentioned that night, and I wondered if Dad remembered it.

"But, sahib, dat is not being da way." Ahmed didn't understand that it was pointless to try to talk my father out of a shortcut.

"Not again," Amy groaned from beside me in the backseat.

The shortcut dead-ended at a small marketplace. There, a variety of small shops popped up, each about as big as a hallway coat closet.

Mom oohed and ahhed and grabbed her sketchpad. "Let's go see what there is here."

Amy and I clambered out behind her. It was almost dusk, and the orange sun slowly died behind us. "You girls go ahead," Dad said, leaning against the car and turning to Ahmed. "So, what's the name of this town? Have you been here before?"

Amy and Mom walked ahead, but I stopped before a shop displaying silver jewelry. I collected charms from everywhere we traveled. The shopkeeper, a round woman dressed in a long-sleeved dress with a scarf over her head flashed a big toothless smile, picked up several necklaces and dangled them before me.

I shook my head and displayed my charm bracelet. "No, something small." I held my fingers out showing about half an inch between my thumb and index finger.

The woman nodded, dug through the pile, and withdrew a small tray loaded with little silver items. My eyes locked on a piece forming some loopy Arabic writing. It would probably turn my wrist green but I could polish it everyday. I picked it up. "How much this?"

The old woman held up ten gnarled fingers and flashed them up and down. "Twenty rupees." *About fifty cents.*

Before I could reply, I felt a tug on my shirt, "No, too much," came a raspy whisper. I glanced over my shoulder and saw the little boy from the mosque.

I whirled around to face him. "Rashid, where did you come from?" He couldn't have walked in the time it took us to drive.

"I am drive," he said. *Drove? How old was he? Ten? And I couldn't drive in a foreign country until I was eighteen. He couldn't have driven. How could he afford a car?* "You say, 'Qeemat ya kafisara kay say.' It mean 'for what money?' You pay ten rupees," he told me. "She want too much."

The woman's smile vanished. She rounded on the small boy and began to shout. He yelled back. Neighboring shopkeepers joined in the fray.

I glanced around, embarrassed. I wanted to sink into the ground, but Rashid didn't back down. He shouted as loudly as the adults. After a long volley of words, the woman nodded her head and waved a hand towards the piece of silver. Rashid turned to me with a big grin, holding up his fingers. "Ten rupee."

As I fumbled for the coins, I saw that Mom and Amy rushed towards me. My face flamed as Mom said, "Ronni, we are visitors in this country. Don't make a spectacle of yourself."

I glanced toward Rashid, but he was gone. *That little kid appeared and disappeared into thin air.* I didn't have a chance to explain the situation.

Mom grabbed my arm. "How about staying with us," she said. "We don't need you starting a riot." The words barely left her mouth when we heard angry shouts behind us.

I looked back, mesmerized. A group of men closed in on something. A shiver of fear crawled down my spine with the memory of a bleeding man with blank eyes. The men shouted angrily; their eyes gleamed with excitement.

Mom pushed us to the side. "This looks like trouble. We need to get around this mess to the car."

But she was too late. Someone else pushed me forward, into the path of the crowd. The crowd seemed to suck me in like quicksand. Terrified, I reached out for Mom. She wasn't there. Neither was Amy. A young girl shoved me. "Al-hamdu-lillah," she said, pointing ahead excitedly.

"What? I don't understand you!" I cried.

The crowd seemed to open for me—inviting me in or forming a trap? Horrified, I saw Rashid. Pale and sweaty, he attempted to pull away from a man. One of the man's hands firmly gripped Rashid's wrist—in the free hand he held a large machete. Shouts from the crowd drowned out the words I saw Rashid's mouth form. *Oh, my God. Rashid.*

"No, no," my cries mingled with the crowd's yells.

I searched for my parents, pushing against the crowd, which attempted to shove and drag me closer towards Rashid. Men in their pajamas and woman covered so only their eyes showed in downward glances surrounded me. I had to get to my father and Ahmed. They had to rescue Rashid from the man with the knife. "Move. Let me go," I screamed. "Get out of my way."

Sweaty faces stared at me with eager, shiny eyes. A little boy held his father's hand, laughing, moving closer to the man with the knife—pushing me closer.

"Murgh-I-mussalam." Another person pushed against me.

"No, excuse me!"

"Al-hamdu-lillah!" Rashid yelled.

I turned to him. "No!" I realized there was no time to get help. I had to make them stop. I stepped out into the center. "Let him go," I yelled.

It became deadly quiet. I spun, stared into every face around the circle; every face stared back at me.

Oh no. What had I done?

I turned back to Rashid. He was gone. A small boy's shirt dangled from the bully's hand. The man threw the shirt down and charged towards me with his knife raised. The crowd glared at me while murmuring among themselves.

I remembered Shirley Jackson's story, "The Lottery." One lady draws the lucky "X" and is stoned to death. *Maybe Rashid had been the human sacrifice, and now that he'd escaped, I had to take his place.* I reeled, searching for a gap, a way out of the circle.

"No, let me go!"

"Murgh-I-mussalam."

The crowd closed in, smothering me. I flung my arms, lashing out, trying to break free. An arm grabbed mine. "No! Let me go!" I yelled. I tried to jerk my arm away, but my assailant spun me around and yanked me away from the circle. I doubled up my fist ready to punch my attacker.

"Little Memsahid, it be okay." Ahmed faced me. He pushed me away from the crowd and toward my dad. I looked over my shoulder to see the man who had held Rashid and several others following us. Their words sounded like a jumble of grunted, gruff sounds.

"Dad! Dad, those people—" I yelled.

"Calm down," my father said, waving his palms towards me. "Ahmed, what's going on?"

"Dat boy, he steal lamb kabob from dis man," Ahmed explained.

"They were going to stab Rashid," I added. "With that knife." I pointed at the man with the machete.

"Sahib, day cut his hand." Ahmed made a slashing motion at his wrist.

"Cut it off?" Dad asked.

"That's sick," I said. "Dad, you remember that little kid at the mosque. He must be hungry. Can't you just pay for the kabob so they won't go after him?"

Dad glanced from the arguing men to Ahmed. "Can I do that, Ahmed?" Why couldn't he? In Morocco, he didn't call the police to help the bloody man. Why couldn't he help Rashid?

Ahmed nodded his head. "If sahib want. It be good."

Dad counted out ten rupees; which I'm sure, was more than the cost of one lousy kabob. We hurried into the Jeep. This time Dad let Ahmed find the way.

We had only driven a few miles when Amy let out a scream. "Back there." Ahmed swerved to a stop, and I turned to see a grinning Rashid, peeking over the back seat.

"Where did you come from?" I asked. "Are you okay?"

Before Rashid could answer, Ahmed flung his door wide, threw open the hatch, and grabbed the boy by the ear, pulling him out of the back.

Rashid spoke rapidly to Ahmed and looked pleadingly at me. I didn't understand him but I knew we wouldn't take him back to the market. "Let him go. We're not taking him back," I said. "Let's take him home."

"No," Ahmed said. "He walk home now." Rashid stared at me, but I dared not speak.

We piled back in the Jeep, and watched as the forlorn figure of Rashid grew smaller and smaller. *Would I ever see that little kid again? Would he be all right? Even though Dad paid for the food, would the Kabob man want revenge?*

Chapter Four

On Mom's orders, Amy and I tromped to the small room we shared. "I don't want you girls waiting until the last minute, then wailing because you can't find something you just have to have for school. Get yourselves together right now," she'd said.

In a matter of minutes, Amy had scooped her stuff together and jammed it into her backpack. She threw her clothing over the desk and chair we shared and flopped on her bed. Soon she hummed to herself as she thumbed through some old magazines. "Boring," she said. "I can't wait for school to start."

I paced the room, gathering supplies, stacking and restacking notebooks and pencils. At last I filled my backpack and sat on the edge of the bed. My hands felt clammy, my stomach in a knot. I reached across the bed and picked up the pair of jeans I would wear. I'd gotten them at the PX in Spain. My curling iron was on the dresser, ready and waiting to do wonders with my hair in the morning. It wasn't enough; I didn't have Shawn or Valeria. *Would I fit in at this new school—I.S.I., the International School of Islamabad?*

The walls seemed to close in on me. I gave Juma a shout and ran down the stairs, grabbing her leash as we headed for the door. "Taking Juma for a walk," I shouted, snapping the leash to her collar.

I closed the door on my mother's, "It's a school night."

Mountains loomed in the darkening background. Dad had explained how interesting it was that we lived under the Himalayas, the highest mountains in the world. Up there, Chinese communists imprisoned Tibetan monks. I imagined the peaks as my personal prison.

Juma and I headed towards the American club with its pool and snack shop. We passed another apartment building, then a smaller brick building of just one story. It lay between the apartment complex and the wall surrounding the American club. I sobbed and Juma looked up at me. Sitting on the curb, I began running my hands through her thick pelt as she washed the tears from my face.

"Do you miss it too, girl?" I asked. "Do you get sick of being dragged from place to place, wherever Dad has to go? Tomorrow is just another day in Morocco. We've been gone almost a week. Have they already forgotten us?" I wiped my eyes on the sleeve of my shirt.

Juma's ears shot up. She turned her head and dashed away from me. "Wait. Come back," I called after her and then I saw him. He was short and wearing brown slacks and the dress shirt of an embassy Marine. He took off his white cap to reveal a red crew cut as Juma jumped on him. "Whoa, a guard dog."

I ran after her, pulling her down off the guy's once clean uniform. "I'm sorry."

"No problem. I'm just getting off guard so it's okay. Are you hiding here in the dark next to my billets ready to break in?"

"What?"

He extended his hand and laughed, I could just make out the patch of freckles across his narrow nose. "I'm Rocky." We shook, then he nodded toward the one-story building between the brick wall blocking off the pool area and the first of the three-story condo-complexes. "This is where I live with the other guys. I haven't seen you around here before, so are you here to clean us out or what?"

Juma pulled on her leash, whining. "Hush girl," I said. *God, what if he'd heard me talking to Juma? How embarrassing.*

I got Juma under control.

"Do you have a name?" he asked.

"Ronni." I glanced over my shoulder as though someone called me. "I have to go." I turned towards the complex.

"Well, Ronni-I-have-to-go, you know it's not all that bad. I have two twin sisters back home in Boston. I miss them everyday." He'd heard me. "When I was your age, I wished I'd been able to travel all over the world. I'd never heard of Islamabad. One day you'll graduate and get to live where ever you want or if you become a Marine, you get sent where ever you're needed."

God, he'd eavesdropped on me. Would he tell the world? "I know," I said, dragging Juma away.

* * *

As I lay awake that night worrying, Amy seemed to sleep totally unfazed. She could kiss her friends goodbye without regret and take it for granted that everyone in the new place waited to meet her. But I had butterflies.

Making new friends was tricky. I could smile at someone else's boyfriend and make an enemy, or talk to a nerd and be forever labeled a geek. *What were Shawn and Valeria doing?*

I thought managing the bus would be easy. All I had to do was sit in the same general area as other kids who appeared to be my age. Every seat toward the back was taken, so I settled for a place toward the middle. Then I found out the O'Malleys had forgotten to give me a vital piece of bus information. A blonde girl with a pony tail leaned over my shoulder and said, "You from Virginia too?" Before I could answer she turned to the girl sitting next to her. "We got more Virginians."

"I'm from Maryland," I admitted.

"Then you're sitting on the wrong side. This is the Virginian side," she said, glaring at me.

I couldn't get up while the bus rolled, so I sat, hot with anger and embarrassment, while the Virginians, whose side of the bus I had accidentally invaded, glared at me until the bus stopped, and I was able to get up and move over. Embassy families always went back to Virginia or Maryland to live because our fathers worked in Washington, D.C. I never encountered a cold war between kids from one state against those from the other. I wasn't sure if there were any rules about talking to Virginians, because no one tells you these things when you're new. You find out the hard way.

The bus stopped in front of four squat brick buildings with thick, white concrete roofs held up by white pillars. Inside, a series of three diamond-shaped quads created a maze. Every room looked the same. Four buildings formed the outside walls to a courtyard containing a star-shaped, tiled concrete depression that resembled a wading pool without any water. Little third-graders sat in one depression eating a snack. *Room 5 . . . didn't I already pass that room twice? Where the heck was 21, anyway?*

I found rooms 20 and 21, ten minutes late, and I had to find the office for a late pass. On the way, I spotted the ladies' room. Afraid I may never find the bathroom again, I decided to duck inside. As I pushed open the door, a teacher came in after me. "Are you a teacher here?" She frowned with her hands on the flowered dress at her wide hips.

Was she blind? "No," I answered. "I'm new."

"Well, you can't be in here. This is for teachers, not children. Go on now."

I didn't have to use the restroom the rest of the day.

My next challenge was locating and opening my locker. The lockers lined the sides of each block of six classrooms. At lunch, instead of eating, I found my locker.

I dialed in the combination—left 24, right 36, left 9. It wouldn't open. Again left, right, left. It didn't budge. "Stupid thing!"

"Need some help?" The clear, low voice startled me.

I spun to see a girl about my age. Her eyes sparkled from beneath thick, black lashes. Her hair was shiny black and styled in a straight neat braid that hung all the way down her back. She wore a loose, long-sleeve shirt and light cotton pants over skin the color of cinnamon. She moved towards my locker like a cat on tiny feet.

If I had to get help with the locker, I'd look stupid. "No, I got it." I swallowed the knot of frustration in my throat.

Left, right, left. Nothing. I mumbled, "I hate this place." I balled up the paper with the combination printed on it. "Left, right, left. Damn it all. I hate it here!" I pounded the locker.

"What's the combination?" she whispered. "I'll try." Her hand brushed my arm.

And just like that, with a friendly word and a gentle touch, the stranger cut the right wire to defuse the bomb. My hand shook as I handed over the crumpled piece of paper.

"You're new, aren't you? I saw you in Mrs. Campbell's English class." She extended her right hand. "My name is Frana. You're an American, no?"

At last, a friendly smile. I shook her hand. "Yes, I'm an American. My name is Ronni . . . ah, Veronica. I got here two days ago."

As Frana dialed in my combination, a boy about my height walked by. He had black hair, dark skin, and surprisingly light hazel eyes; he was stocky, like a weightlifter, but moved with an easy grace.

"You looking at him?" Frana asked.

I automatically grabbed for my half heart wondering how she'd seen with her back turned. *Okay cute, but I still loved Shawn. Would Shawn look at another girl? What if I never saw Shawn again? Would I be alone forever?* I wasn't sure what to say. For all I knew the boy was the class chump. "Uhm, no. Well, I don't know. Maybe?"

Frana giggled. "That's Luke. He's a freshman like us. You probably have him in all your classes. There are only about twenty of us—freshmen, I mean." I noticed Ian in all of my classes and that he always had different girls sitting on either side of him.

Frana struck my locker above the lock, and the door flew open. "There," she said with a smile. "Most of the locks stick."

"Thanks." I studied her as I stowed my books.

Frana obviously wasn't an American. In fact, she was probably a native, but she seemed okay.

"What are you doing for lunch?" she asked.

I traced a poster plastered on the wall next to my locker, avoiding her eyes. I didn't know how long I was going to be in Pakistan. If I made friends I'd have more people to say goodbye to. No one could replace Valeria or Shawn. "I don't know."

"You interested in the cultural exchange?" she asked.

"What?"

"The poster." I looked more closely. It announced a cultural exchange with Kabul, Afghanistan. "Actors, Athletes, Singers, and Artists wanted. Come represent your school."

"I'm playing soccer, and I play the piano. I think tryouts are over, but they need prop people and scenery painters. If you're interested," she said.

I looked back at the sign. The trip was in a week and we moved into our new house that weekend. Mom would never agree to the trip.

*   *   *

At dinner that night, Dad asked, "So how was school?"

Amy shrugged and took a bite of her hamburger. I hesitated a minute before saying, "There's a cultural exchange in Kabul, Afghanistan next week and I met the Iranian Ambassador's daughter, Frana. She asked me if I wanted to go. She says they need set designers and props people."

"Afghanistan?" Dad asked. "You'll be interested to learn that Afghanistan is full of history. The Russians have been fighting for control there for years."

Oh no, not another history lesson. "Come on, Dad. They aren't going to kill us. Can't I go?"

"I suppose. It isn't dangerous and it might be an interesting experience for you." He grabbed for a homemade biscuit, cut it, and reached for the butter.

"It's out of the question," Mom said with a quick glare at Dad. "I need you girls to help me unpack and set up the house."

"No," my dad said. "I think we should let her go. It's a great opportunity. We have a cook and bearer, plus I can hire some additional help."

"You always let her get out of all her responsibilities," Mom argued, but in the way she did when she knew she had no argument.

I was going to Kabul. And so were Ian and Frana. Not that I cared about that. Thank goodness, I didn't have to stand around being yelled at by Mom all week.

That weekend, we moved to our house, number 24 Nara Road. It was the last house on a street that began with a field of red and yellow poppies. Dad said the people grew poppies to harvest for their opium.

Next to the poppy field, a tin and mud shack stood. The day we arrived, two men sat outside the shack holding hands. Two other men hugged and kissed nearby. I looked at my parents to see if they had noticed, but they didn't say a word.

"What's that?" I asked Dad.

"It's a tea house. At the end of the day the men buy their tea, smoke, and relax. It's against the law to drink alcohol in an Islamic country."

"You drink and you're in an Islamic nation." I said.

"I'm not Islamic," he countered.

Our house towered two stories high with a large living room for entertaining foreign dignitaries. Amy and I had our own rooms across from one another on the second floor.

All weekend, Mom had us lugging dusty Persian carpets in and moving them around until they were just right. We moved bulky wooden furniture from one side of the room to the other whenever she got a whim. The couch started out under the window but had to be moved. Side tables like bookends framed the couch and Mom's artwork from Morocco and Africa hung on the white plaster walls.

The dining room sunk below the living room, three steps down. I almost fell lugging leafs to the dining room table down those steps. Mom set up her art studio in a large alcove off the dining room. She unfolded two bulky, wooden, intricately carved screens to shield the studio from the dining room. Two wide white swinging doors separated the dining room from the kitchen.

I could just imagine the cook, Akbar, bustling through those doors carrying Mom's brass tea set when Mom hosted one of her ladies bridge parties. At Mom's ladies parties, Juma sniffed around, trying to steal some of the triangularly shaped tuna and egg salad sandwiches.

By dinnertime Sunday, I was dead tired. Because one of the legs was missing from the dining room table, Mom set up a card table in the kitchen in order to eat our ham sandwiches for dinner.

Amy chattered away about a cockroach she'd seen and claimed was as big as her hand. I thought about the red bugs I watched Akbar sift from the flour before making the bread and hoped they weren't baby cockroaches.

"I can't believe my dining room table leg is missing, and we still have so much unpacking to do," Mom complained. "I don't see how we can let Ronni go to Kabul when the house is such a mess." Before Dad could answer, a rap sounded at the door. The bearer, Mohammed, went to answer it and came back trailing a small figure. The figure stepped forward and I recognized little Rashid from the market place.

"Runny, I work you." He stared at me.

"What are you doing here?" I asked as Juma nuzzled up to him, sniffing at his dirty hands. Rashid moved away from her and circled the bearer who shooed the dog away. Rashid stayed hidden behind the bearer while Juma continued to try to tickle him with her nose and tongue. Mohammed almost fell keeping the two apart.

"We have all the help we need," Mom said "And besides you stole a kabob and you're filthy." Mohammed finally got a hold of Juma's collar and disappeared to put her in the guestroom. Her excited yipping was muted behind the closed door.

Rashid safely emerged and stood before us, smiling broadly. I looked at Dad. "Give him a chance. You said you needed more help with unpacking and he can always wash his hands."

"Fine. You're hired, but you need to bathe and clean under your nails," Dad said.

"You aren't touching my food," Amy announced.

"James, you didn't even discuss it with me," Mom protested.

"You needed more help—now you have it." Dad smiled and winked at me.

Chapter Five

Two mornings later, Ahmid dropped me off at school. Frana stood by the yellow school bus that trailed a billow of black exhaust. She ran over and dropped her small red suitcase on the ground next to my backpack.

I glanced at her bag with a sinking feeling, regretting my lack of anything fancier than blue jeans. "Oh no, we aren't going to have to dress up are we?"

"I bought a dress for my piano recital, but other than that I doubt it." She grabbed my hand and pulled me on the bus behind Danny East, who opened his mouth revealing crackers stuck in his braces and falling out of his mouth as he pushed his face in that of Katie Leonard's. Katie flipped her glossy shoulder-length hair off her shoulder and grimaced at the idiot. "Go bug someone else."

On the bus, Katie, the prettiest girl in our class, smiled at Ian and glided into the seat next to him. Frana maneuvered us into a seat directly in front of them. Of course Ian would like Katie. She always knew just how to wear her makeup and when to toss her hair.

As Ian winked at me, my cheeks flamed. I realized I still stood gaping at them. Turning, I plopped down next to Frana.

We rode east toward Kabul. Several spitballs flew through the air and hit Luke who sat two rows ahead of us on the other side. He spun around and glared at Danny who lowered a straw. "I'm going kill you if you don't cut it out," Luke growled, flexing his biceps.

Danny shrugged. "Not me." Luke scooted out of his seat to get to

Danny. I spun around to catch the fight when two large trucks rolled by, catching my attention. Bright pictures of a wild tiger and an elephant sprang from the surface of one truck. "Is that a circus?" I asked Frana as I tilted my head to peer around Ian, who stood between Luke and Danny.

"Excuse me," Frana said. "Luke, why don't you sit down before the driver stops and kicks you off?" He sunk into the seat.

Then she pointed out the window. "No, the drivers spend tons of money to get their trucks painted. It's a status symbol. Only the rich truck owners can paint their trucks." I stared at the high arc of the truck with metal trim and mosque-like elegant curved top. I examined the other truck, which depicted a garden scene with flowers, trees, and bird in the same vivid colors. A sign hung on the side: God is one, Allah.

"The sign's in English," I noted.

"Yes, another example of showing off. Much like the boys," she said, pointing to Ian in the process of losing an arm wrestling contest with Luke.

Luke slammed down his hand, winning the competition. Cute and strong. He caught me staring, and I peered at the other truck and caught two more signs one read: "Take your own chances". What did that mean? What chance should I take? The other sign read, "Do your own thing." Whatever that was. Weird.

The rest of the traffic varied as much as it had on the ride from the airport—with water buffalos, bikes, pedestrians, and vehicles. A green bus with men hanging out the window pulled beside us. The men jeered and made faces at us. Ian's hand grazed my hair as he slid back into his seat. "Sorry," he whispered into my ear so that his smoky breath tickled the side of my face. Was he flirting with me?

An hour later, we stopped in the middle of a bazaar with a large white plaster archway at the end. Beyond the archway rested the Khyber

Pass, the passageway between Pakistan and Afghanistan. Beneath the white arc, buses sputtered and belched clouds of black exhaust. Frayed ropes secured crates and cardboard boxes to the tops of the buses in piles so high they teetered as the vehicles bumped forward.

One of the teacher-chaperons, Mrs. Cook, pushed at a bobby pin in her graying hair coiled in a tight bun at her neck and announced, "The Khyber Pass is the voiceless witness to most of the invasions of the subcontinent."

Ian leaned against my shoulder and whispered, "Oh no, watch out, we're going to get a history lesson." I wanted to add, *you should live with my dad,* but didn't.

Instead I giggled as Mrs. Cook continued. "The Aryans, the Persians, and then, in 326 B.C., Alexander the Great." Maybe Ian didn't really like Katie because it was me he whispered to. Several students yawned, and she added, "This is the only rest stop for miles. Get off and use the bathroom in the American guesthouse. Don't wander away."

Frana got up and I followed her. Ian pushed me past her, and we stepped off the bus. I watched the group go one way while we went the other. But Mrs. Cook didn't notice as she waddled to the side of the road, clasping Danny's ear in one pudgy hand while saying, "Young man, we don't put gum in people's seats."

"I'm Persian. Where's my piece of Afghanistan?" Frana joked.

"I'm Greek; like Alexander the Greek," Ian said.

"It's Alexander the Great," I corrected him.

"That's just because someone misunderstood the Greek part back then," he insisted.

"More like Alexander the Geek." I laughed, picking my way through the flea market-like place filled with the beckoning of vendors hawking everything from fabric to fish.

"Shut up," he said, draping his arms around our shoulders and steering us into a store with walls made up of large metal shipping crates. Frana shrugged his shoulder off. We passed little stands selling dates and chilies and more selling pipes and jewelry.

"Make me." I moved away from his shoulder, too.

"Okay." He leaned over and kissed me hard on the mouth. He tasted like chewing gum and bacon. I felt dizzy when he pulled away. Before I could respond, he grabbed my hand and pulled me farther into the store. My head reeled from the kiss. Maybe he really liked me. But what if it was just a joke? I didn't kiss him. I wouldn't do that to Shawn. Shawn kissed great.

"Mrs. Cook said not to go far from the bus," Frana warned as I glanced at her to see what she thought about Ian kissing me. She looked straight ahead. Maybe she didn't see.

"She doesn't have to know," Ian continued to lead us into the shop. The dark, mustached, sinister-looking proprietors wore bullet-studded bandoleers and smoked foreign cigars. Were these guys the kind who shot people for no reason? The picture of a bloody man with blank eyes forced its way into my mind and I shook my head as though shaking the image out.

Nervously, I glanced around the concave crate walls covered with netting. In each cavity hung sleek semi-automatic weapons, piles of hand grenades, and enough anti-aircraft munitions to start a war. Ian looked around and asked to check out a machine gun. "Hey, look, U.S. serial numbers," he said, holding it aloft. "Can I buy one of these?"

One of the vendors approached Ian, "You have many rupees?"

They weren't really going to sell Ian a weapon? Were they? How did they get U.S. weapons? We couldn't defend ourselves against the dangerous men. "Let's go," I clutched Frana's hand and backpedaled out of the store. "They might decide we're target practice."

As we approached the bus, I noticed a small dark boy standing next to it arguing with the driver. "Rashid?"

"Runny," he called. "You need guide? I go Kabul, you?"

"What are you doing here, Rashid?" I turned to Frana. "This is the little kid I told you about."

"I go you," Rashid said, apparently ignoring my question.

"No. You can't. This trip is with my school. Where'd you come from anyway?" I spun my head around to look for a bus or something. Was he following me? And if he was, how had he gotten to the pass?

"I go," Rashid persisted.

Katie shook her head towards me as she scooted on the bus, passed by Ian, and muttered "Not another beggar."

Mrs. Cook called us. I turned to Rashid. "How much rupees for a bus back home?" I asked him.

"Five." He held up the fingers on one hand—the same hand that he'd almost lost. I remembered hearing if you saved someone you became responsible for them. Fishing out five notes, I handed them to him and got a glimpse over his shoulder to see a woman.

Only her eyes showed behind dark lashes, a veil, headdress, and equally dark clothes. Three dirty children clung to her and she held little packs of Chiclets out, not venturing too close to the bus. What a way to make a living. Katie's words "Not another beggar," came back to me. I marched over to the mother, dug out three more rupees and handed them to her. She tried to give me all her merchandise but I took one, spun around, found Katie's face in the window, and smiled at her.

I handed the gum to Rashid and pointed to the bus. "Go home, now." I entered the bus, and as I waved goodbye to the little kid with the pleading face, the bus chugged beneath the archway and entered the

Khyber Pass behind one of the overloaded lopsided buses. Natives hung out of its door and windows. The right rear tire looked like it belonged to a tricycle while the left one looked like a tractor wheel.

The trip to Kabul took forever. The bus twisted and turned on the two-lane road, which cut through mountains 11,000 feet above sea level. Camels lumbered on the peaks high above us. I stole a glance at Ian. He winked. *Why had he kissed me? He had a girlfriend, so why flirt with me?*

When we arrived at the American School in Kabul, a family called the Smiths took Frana and me home to stay with them for the week. They lived in a white two-story house, a block from the U.S. Embassy on a main road to the Afghan president's house.

We weren't going to stay there a week; as it turned out. The next day, Frana stayed late at the American School to help me glue leaves on a piece of scenery. We nearly finished when Ian rushed into the auditorium, crushing a cigarette out on the floor and flashing a bottle of champagne from under his jacket. "Look what I got from the teacher's reception." He took a swig and handed it to me.

I drank half a beer once even though I hated the flavor. Beer made my grandfather beat my grandmother and made me feel sick. But, I wiped the neck of the bottle and took a gulp. It burned my throat as it slid down. I had to cover my mouth to keep it down. The stuff tasted bitter. I held the bottle out to Frana. "I can't," she said. "I'm a Muslim." I passed it back to Ian.

He took another gulp, sat down and gave me a sly look. "Okay, so what'll you give me if I help you glue leaves?" He passed me the bottle again and dipped a leaf in the glue.

I took a deep swig to avoid the question and my answer. *What did he want from me? What did I want from him?* I loved Shawn. Shawn was the cutest guy I ever met. Ian could make me laugh though. Plus, he wasn't a million miles away. Our ride arrived at 5:00.

When we got to the Smith's house, I felt sick from the liquor. I went up to the room and flopped on my bed. The room spun and the air throbbed. I heard a plane roar overhead and then another. Gunfire pierced the air. "What's that?" I staggered to the window.

Frana raced in as a flash of lights penetrated the gauzy curtains. Something sizzled. A crash shook the house. *What the heck? Were we under attack?*

Automatic weapon fire rattled, and voices shouted in Afghani.

"Who's shooting? What are they saying?" I asked Frana.

"They're yelling, 'run, go,'" she said.

Terrified, but eaten up with curiosity, I crawled to the window and inched back the curtains. A plane roared past and dropped something onto a nearby building. It exploded in a flash of flame and billow of smoke. The window rattled. Dust rose from the rubble where the building once stood. Oh, my God, the whole thing blew up. I heard the plane again. Were we next?

Frana grabbed my arm and pulled me away from the vibrating window. "Let's go," she yelled. *Go where?* I thought.

We ran down the stairs, and found Mr. Smith with the phone to his ear. His wife and daughter huddled next to him. He motioned us toward the back of the house. "The American Embassy says it's an attack," he called. "A Soviet-led coup. Stay at ground level and keep away from the windows."

Outside, people ran past. Gunshots echoed and bullets ricocheted off the garage. A woman with an infant in her arms dashed into the street. She staggered, twisted, and fell. "Oh, my God," I said in horror. "They're killing people out there. The lady and her baby. We have to get help."

"No! Stay inside." Mr. Smith seized my arm. "You'll be killed." Mrs. Smith shoved me away from the window and a second later the glass smashed. Lethal shards of glass sprayed in all directions. I screamed and ran.

We huddled on the floor in the center of the family room. Bullets hummed and zinged as they struck the walls. Tracers streaked bright across the darkening sky. Gigi Smith, a year younger than I, clung to her father. "This can't be happening. Why is the Soviet Union attacking us?"

"They aren't attacking us. They want a communist leader in power," Mr. Smith informed her.

A crash shook the house and plaster fell from around the chandelier. The lights flickered and went out. "They have to stop. We're going to die," Gigi cried. "Why are they doing this? It isn't their country."

I squeezed Frana's hand. She gave me a weak smile and squeezed mine in return.

Mr. Smith crawled to the phone. "The line's dead," he said. Another bomb exploded, and we ducked our head to avoid chunks of flying plaster. "All we can do is wait and see," Mr. Smith said, brushing himself off.

"We have to hide. We have to get out of here," Gigi said. *We couldn't get home, not through bullets and bombs.*

"This is unreal. I don't want to die yet," I whispered.

"Neither do I. I want to go home," Frana said.

"I wish I'd never come," I said, wondering what Shawn, Dad, Mom, and Amy were doing.

"I'm sorry." She touched my arm.

"It's not your fault. This is crazy. They're killing people in the street." I stood up, agitated, and started to pace. We had to get out before the whole house blew up.

"We can't do anything but wait now. Sit down with me," Frana said. I huddled next to her.

Gigi cried and screamed, "We're going to die. We're going to die."

"No, honey, it's okay. Sh . . ." Mrs. Smith offered water and a tiny pill. "Here, take this and relax." Gigi took the pill. *What was that?*

"Do they know about this at home?" I whispered.

"They'll know," Frana said. "My father'll call the Iranian Embassy. Or he'll drive here to get me." *Would Frana's father make it through the long pass? What about all those guns and grenades we saw before we entered the pass?*

I wondered if my family would care if I died. If I died, they'd have one child, Amy. Would they even miss me? I felt a fat tear run down my cheek. *Shawn would miss me. He'd care. Would he visit my grave? If a bomb hit the house and I blew into a thousand pieces, would I even have a grave?*

Mrs. Smith handed us a flashlight and two peanut butter sandwiches. "Eat something, girls. Keep your strength up. Everything will be all right," I knew she was lying. She guided a morsel of sandwich to her daughter's mouth. "Eat, honey. It's going to be okay."

"No, it won't," Gigi gasped between sobs. I tried a bite of the sandwich, but I couldn't force the tasteless, sticky lump down my throat.

Frana rose, turned and looked behind me into a dim corner. *What was she looking at?* I spun, expecting to see a soldier pointing a gun at us. I switched on my flashlight and raked the beam across the wall. I saw nothing. Frana knelt and touched her forehead to the floor. "What's wrong?" I asked.

"Sh . . . I'm praying," she said.

Praying? Should I do that? I could pray real—hard, maybe God would let us live. Maybe the bullets would stop. Would God listen to me?

Frana kissed the ground. *Was she praying to the same God? What was Frana praying for? Would God listen to her?*

After a few minutes, Frana crept back to where I crouched. "Do you think there really is a God?" I whispered.

"Of course," she whispered back, holding my hand.

"I drank that champagne. Do you think if we do things we know are wrong, we still get into heaven?"

"We do the best we can. Allah is good, Ronni." She stroked my hair. "He forgives us," she assured me.

"If he lets us live, I'll never drink again. I swear to God."

"Don't swear to God. Promise yourself," Frana said. *Maybe we'd get out of the mess.* I squeezed Frana's arm.

We sat in the dark and I started to hum the theme song to the *Love Boat*. Frana laughed and joined me as I tried to drown out the shouts, screams, and shots. Mr. Smith held Mrs. Smith, who rocked Gigi back and forth in her arms. I tried not to think that at any minute someone might burst through the door with a gun, but I couldn't keep my mind on anything else.

"We need to cross the street to the American Embassy," Mr. Smith said during a lull in the attack. "They have a generator. Plus, they have the Marines."

Yes, I thought. The Marines had guns and the embassy had a gate. *But crossing the street? The same street with all the shooting and screaming?*

"There are dead people out there. We won't make it," Gigi whimpered.

"It's quieter now. We have to try," Mr. Smith said.

I grabbed Frana's hand. "Come on. Let's get our bags. I need my ID."

"Be careful," Mrs. Smith warned. "Stay away from the windows."

We crunched over broken glass and up the stairs. I kept the flashlight beam low to the ground so no one would see it from the outside. The shredded curtains in the bedroom whipped in the night wind and the smell of explosives stung my nose. Someone cried. Someone else moaned.

I wanted to peer over the window ledge to see. How many dead bodies lay in the road? Did someone need help? But, I didn't dare go near the window. A rumble traveled down the streets and the house shook. I stood on the bed and saw the road. One tank and then another rolled down the street, flattening bodies and rubble.

"Tanks," I whispered. Bursts of gunshots interrupted me. Fire escaped from the gun port of a tank and something exploded, knocking me to the floor. The room spun and my ears stopped working. *Was I hit? Was I dying*? Patting myself, I still had both legs. I didn't hurt anywhere except my back where hard sharp things cut into my shirt.

Frana's lips moved but I heard no words. She reached down to help me up. The house shook again. I grabbed my backpack and fled the room.

Back in the family room, we waited. I needed to pee but I was afraid to leave the room. My hearing gradually returned; I could hear occasional spurts of gunfire, but I couldn't judge the distance. After a while, Mr. Smith said, "Okay, let's cross the street."

"Are the tanks gone?" I asked.

"I can't hear them," Mrs. Smith replied.

Mr. Smith went to the door first, followed by Frana and me. Mrs. Smith tugged Gigi behind us. "We can't go," Gigi yelled. "Don't open the door, please."

"It's all right, honey," Mrs. Smith said pushing her along.

"No, it's not!"

"Get her to quiet down," Mr. Smith ordered. "Before someone hears us."

"I don't think I can give her another Valium," Mrs. Smith said.

"Well, put your hand over her mouth. Okay, turn off your flashlight." He flipped his own and let the light flow over one and then the other of us.

As Mr. Smith opened the door, smoke rose through the darkness, assaulting my nostrils. It almost covered the metallic smells of shell casings, blood, and sweat. I couldn't see a thing. Not one streetlight illuminated our way. A burst of light shot across the sky and lit up a clutter of bodies and debris. Something exploded nearby. "What was that?" I flinched.

"Nothing. Everything's okay," Frana said.

Frana and I clung together as we scampered across the street. On the far side, I tripped over something—a body? If I stared straight ahead, I wouldn't see any people. Frana pulled me on. We ran again, and I stubbed my toe on something hard. It throbbed with more pain than the glass in my back. We pushed on.

The embassy stood across the street and on the next block. We rushed towards it. A bullet zinged past the fence on my left. I froze and fell to my knees dragging Frana with me. Gigi screamed, "We're going to die. We're going to die." I staggered to my feet and fled, pulling Frana at my side.

"I can't move. I can't," Gigi whined. "I've been hit. They shot me."

"Gigi. Be quiet," Mr. Smith ordered. He doubled back and picked her up. Another bullet whanged off something in the middle of the street. Mr. Smith, Gigi in his arms, ran ahead of us.

The embassy guard booth had been smashed and the locked gate bent inward. A hole gaped at one side of the iron gate where the tanks had probably bashed into it. *Had a rebel gotten in to lay in wait for us?* In the distance, a rumbling began again. Mr. Smith put Gigi down. "We're almost there, honey."

We crawled in the dirt through the hole. Once inside, we dashed for the embassy. The rumbling behind us grew louder. My lungs burned. Shots came from everywhere. Mr. Smith pounded on the embassy door.

"Who's there?" a fearful voice came from inside.

"It's Reggie Smith with A.I.D. Let us in! Let us in! My daughter's been shot."

The glass security door opened, and we entered a metal room with a big metal door at the end, closest to the rest of the embassy. Two guards peered at us through a hole and asked Mr. Smith to put his identification up to the window. The window rattled, and we hit the floor. Gigi's blood-soaked jeans clung to her calf.

When the tanks passed, we each stood beside the window so the Marines could view us. "Is she an Afghani?" One Marine pointed at Frana.

"No, the Iranian Ambassador's daughter," Mr. Smith said. "The girls are here from Islamabad, Pakistan, with a school trip. I need medical attention for my daughter."

The Marine opened the door. "Sorry, Mr. Smith. I didn't recognize you. Hell of a night."

He escorted us to the basement where a dozen other people sat in the semi-dark. Frana and I joined the Smiths in the corner. "What's the news?" Mr. Smith asked.

"The president's dead. Killed. The communists are in power," a man in a torn suit told us.

"What does that mean? What's going to happen to us?" I asked.

Mr. Smith patted my arm. "We wait. But don't be scared—the Soviet

Union won't create an international incident by coming after us."

Frana and I huddled together, listening to distant noises. Gigi whimpered in the corner, nursing her bandaged leg. No one slept.

"I've never seen a dead person before," I told Frana. "I want to pray for the lady and baby and all the others who've been killed."

"Yes," Frana said. "For peace and a safe return home, too."

We camped out for three days in the embassy basement. We had a generator for power, but there wasn't much to eat or drink besides cans of soda and saltine crackers.

On the fourth day, the school bus arrived at the embassy. When we got on, I saw the seats had been removed and a dozen bullets had hit the bus. "Pile your suitcases and backpacks to the sides of the bus so if we're shot at, the bullets go through the luggage first," Mrs. Cook told us.

I wondered nervously how bulletproof my pajamas and hair dryer would be. Frana eyed the luggage, too.

"Ronni, Frana, over here." I spotted Ian at the back of the bus. He gave us each a big hug. I hugged him back. *Was he just being friendly or did he like me?* His warm shirt was dirty and smelled of sweat and I wondered if I smelled the same. The bus was crowded, so everyone had made it. I tried to get comfortable sitting on the grooves of the bus floor.

Mr. Fox, another teacher, entered the bus with his Afghan hound. "They won't let me take him out of the country. So I'm hiding him on the bus," he explained. Ian got the dog to sit behind us.

"Don't look out the windows and don't stand up," Mrs. Cook warned as the bus started up. "We're heading back to Pakistan. Sardar Mohammed Daoud Khan, the president of Afghanistan, was murdered. I don't need to tell you this is a very serious situation." I thought about the store with the walls of metal shipping crates and all those weapons. Did the rebels have those guns?

"Oh, God." Ian swiped his hand over his forehead. "There are dead people hanging on the fence."

I averted my eyes.

When I lived in Nigeria, they hanged criminals on the beach. I accidentally came upon one of the executions on television and had nightmares for weeks after. But this was no show. I hid my eyes in Ian's shoulder and let the warmth of his arm comfort me without worrying about how Ian felt about me.

When we got to the head of the Khyber Pass, a guard stopped the bus and the driver leaned out the window to speak to him.

Trembling, I hoped we'd get out. The guard might be a communist or think we were. "The dog," Ian said, standing and quickly moving two suitcases in front of the beast moments before the guard entered the bus.

"We won't let them take our political prisoner," he announced.

The guard walked a few steps on the bus and I held my breath. He turned to leave. The dog let out a yelp; the guard turned back. Ian yelped, "Ouch, my hand. She sat on my hand." He pointed at me.

The guard turned to leave. The dog barked. Ian groaned, "Oh, I feel sick!" The guard stared at Ian who leaned against the bags gagging.

I held my breath until the guard got off the bus. Then we all let out a nervous laugh. Thank God, we were all going home alive, even the dog.

We rolled through the Khyber Pass. Mrs. Cook told us, "Afghani rebels are hiding in the hills." I worried we'd be shot at by accident and began to shiver.

Ian belted out "One hundred bottles of beer on the wall." The dog howled.

Little by little other voices joined in, "Ninety-nine bottles of beer." The bus snaked through the pass. We got the bottles off the wall and sang them back up again.

When we reached Pakistan, we all cheered. At the school, Frana's family waited next to my mom. Ian's girlfriend rushed the bus and threw herself at him as he climbed down the steps. I waved goodbye to Frana, and Ian winked at me.

Mom hugged me and said, "We're so glad you're home. We were worried to death." She steered me towards the car and we got in. "Well, at least you lost some weight. I had the cook make your favorite roast chicken, mashed potatoes, and chocolate chip cookies." Wow, mom was concerned about me; maybe she did care.

I looked out the back window and watched Jennifer grab Ian's hand and lead him towards a car where a woman with Ian's red hair hugged them both.

"Mom, did a letter come for me?"

"No."

I had received a letter from Shawn a week and a half before. We had promised to write weekly, and I needed some word from him. I wanted to stop thinking about Ian and his girlfriend.

That night I sat down to the first meal in four days that wasn't saltine crackers and Seven-Up. "So, you had an interesting experience. Did you see bombs being dropped on the Afghan President's house?" Dad asked.

I nodded feeling like a celebrity. Rashid refilled my water glass slowly and hung around for longer than necessary.

As I reached for my third chocolate chip cookie, Mom said, "Ronni, don't be a pig. Two cookies are enough," Bursting the bubble of goodwill I had associated with her. Embarrassed, I put the third cookie back, as Amy stuck her tongue out at me.

Chapter Six

Summer seemed to drag on with swimming and waiting to hear from Shawn and Valeria, my best friends.

"Dad," I called as he entered the door. "Any mail for me?"

"Yes, one letter here." He held it out, and I rushed down the stairs. I snatched it out of his hand and looked at the return address. Valeria wrote. Yes, I needed to talk to someone because Frana had been in Delhi, India with her family for three weeks and would not be back until later that night.

The letter read: "Dear Ronni, school's out for the summer. What are you doing? I went to Zina's pool party. It wasn't the same without you. It's not going to be the same starting our sophomore year. I'm going to Rome for a month this summer. Something happened at the party. I saw Shawn kissing Zina." I dropped the letter. *Shawn kissed Zina? No way.*

My father placed his keys on the shelf under the white birdcage that never held a bird and shuffled his mail. *He ruined my life. He caused Shawn to give up on me.*

"See what you did?" I rattled the paper in his face. "I hate this stupid place," I muttered.

"What's wrong?" Dad asked.

"You forced us to leave Morocco." I glared at him. "We can't stay anywhere. I wanted to stay with Shawn and Valeria, but you always force us to leave. I wish you weren't my father."

Mom turned the corner and Amy followed behind her. "What are you yelling about?" she asked me.

"Because of you guys, my life stinks." I bolted for the stairs taking two at a time. "Because of you guys, Shawn is dating Zina. I hate you both."

"Ronni, calm down," my mom said to my back. "Everyone makes sacrifices." I heard her footsteps behind me. "I had an art show in Morocco and the royal family wanted me to do their portrait—" Her voice trailed off as I slammed the door to my room.

She yelled from outside my room, "Don't slam that door, young lady! You act like a big baby! Beside it was just puppy love! It—" I pressed my pillow to my ears, drowning her out.

I hated them. I dropped the pillow and picked up the brown teddy bear on my bed. It held a heart with the words "I love you" on it. Shawn had given it to me on Valentines Day with a card and scented soaps. I put it to my nose and breathed in the strawberry scent. Then I threw it across the room. Lies, all lies.

He'd written two letters; that was all. I took the letters out of my scrapbook, balled them up, and threw them across the room. Lies, no one ever stuck by your side. They claimed to love you until you moved.

I went to my jewelry box on the dresser to count my getaway money. If I had enough I could get on a plane and go home. He'd break up with Zina when I got back to Morocco. I stopped to look at myself in the mirror. Another bump rose on my cheek. I looked hideous. I opened my mouth and inspected my braces—metal mouth. The only good thing about me was the color of my eyes. But Mom refused to let me wear any eyeliner, so I couldn't even accentuate them. Anyone could easily forget my face. I didn't mean anything to anybody.

I picked up the half heart Shawn gave me. As I ripped it from my neck, I heard a knock on the door and someone opened it. Rashid stood there. "Runny, you okay?"

I wiped a tear from my eye and said. "Yes, Rashid. I just want to be alone for a while." I almost threw the necklace across the room, but I stopped. It was the only reminder that I once meant something to someone. I put it in my jewelry box.

I locked my door and stayed in my room until Frana called at six. I went by my dad's study and saw him reading a newspaper. I hesitated by the door. "If it isn't too much trouble, can I get a ride to Frana's?" I grumbled. "I want to spend the night." I averted my eyes to the carpet. I wasn't forgiving him, no way.

"If your mom says it's all right."

Mom gladly agreed because she and Dad were going to play bridge at the mansion of A.Q. Khan, some Pakistan nuclear engineer, and his Dutch wife. Mom rejoiced at my departure from the house. My dad offered to drive me over to the Iranian Ambassador's house. I didn't say anything to him on the ride. We had nothing to say to each other. He'd ruined my life and I told him I hated him. My head felt stuffed up with anger and guilt.

Silently, Dad waited while I mounted the stairs to the double front door. I struck the door with the large brass knocker and Frana's mom came to the door, smiling. She waved at my dad as I entered the wide hallway. "Ronni, we're so glad you could come," she said in a throaty foreign accent. My feet sunk into colorful, wall-to-wall Persian carpets that covered the floor. Frana descended the wide staircase and hugged me. We hustled up steps under the watchful eyes from a portrait of the Shah of Iran and his wife.

Once in Frana's room, I closed the door. "Shawn is dating this girl I hate," I told her.

"I'm sorry," she said putting her arm over my shoulders.

"I want to go back to Morocco and get him back." I slumped onto her bed. "I miss my old friends. Everyone's moved on like I was never there."

She put a paper bag on my lap. "What is it?" I asked as I lifted it. The object inside the bag was heavy and round.

"It's a gift from India."

I opened the bag and slipped a sturdy metal bracelet from the paper.

"I visited Amritsar. It's a Sikh bracelet," Frana said. "I got it at the Golden Temple." I looked at it without any expression. It looked pretty plain to me. "The Sikhs are like Hindus. It's a symbol of determination. I have one and I got that one for you. We can wear them in honor of our friendship."

If a Muslim could wear one so could I. I slipped it on my wrist. I imagined us wearing our bracelets when we graduated together from I.S.I. and went on to the same college.

She told me about visiting the Taj Mahal and the market place in Delhi. Then she handed me another gift. It was a tiny red seed no bigger than the nail on my pinky finger. An intricately carved ivory sliver of an elephant, approximately the same size as the seed sat on top.

She took it from my fingers, opened it, and poured eight tiny slivers of carved ivory elephants from the inside of the seed into my palm. "An elephant seed?" I asked.

"Yes but if you plant it you don't get an elephant, sorry. And you never know how many you get. Like a Chinese fortune cookie or like life. You get what you get." You get what you get in life. I got the life of a nomad. Never really knowing a home. Never able to hold on to the people I love.

We spread out on Frana's double bed which had a dozen pillows embroidered with what looked like different scenes from some love story. "Do you ever have nightmares about Kabul?" I asked. "Like we're back there or that it happens right here in Pakistan?"

"Yes. Sometimes," Frana answered.

That night before I fell asleep, I fingered the bracelet, watching the silver glint in the dim light from the window. Wearing it made me feel connected to Frana. As long as I wore it, we'd be linked—like salt and pepper, like toast and butter, like Starsky and Hutch. I wanted us to be together always. "Frana," I whispered into the dark.

I heard the rustle of her sheets and then a soft grunt, "Um?"

"When we graduate, where do you want to go to college?"

"Oxford," she said without hesitating.

Oxford? I thought that was a type of shoe, but didn't want to appear ignorant. "Where's that exactly?" I fished for information. "How far is it from here?"

"Not too far." Her voice was thick with sleep. "It's in England."

England. That was good. I wouldn't have to learn a new language. I plumped my pillow. "That sounds great. We'll go together."

"It's a deal," she murmured. "Now, go to sleep."

"Okay."

But I didn't sleep right away. I lay awake, planning how we'd furnish our apartment at Oxford, the double dates we'd go on, the double wedding we'd have, and the houses we'd buy next door to each other. Nothing, I thought as I twirled the bracelet on my wrist, would ever come between us. Or would it?

Chapter Seven

Friday night, a month into my sophomore year, as Frana sat on my bed, I paced around the room. Luke had asked me to the movies. "I want you to come. It's not a date!"

I emphasized the point with my hands. "We're just friends. God, everyone wants to make a big deal out of it," I rambled, but my stomach still tingled when I thought of how cute Luke was.

"Yeah, right. We're just friends. Don't make me laugh," Frana said.

"Believe what you want."

"I don't want to butt in on your date."

"It's not a date. I wouldn't date anyone. Too many people would be in my business. He's okay, but it's not a date." I hated when adults said things like "How cute, your little date." It was as if you were a baby, and they couldn't possibly take you seriously.

"Okay. Okay. Sorry." She plumped a pillow and watched me try on different shirts. I looked awful in all of them. We both wore our Sikh bracelets but I couldn't decide on what jeans and shirt to put on with it.

"If we were in the States, I could get my license in four months. Then I wouldn't have to get Mom to drive everywhere."

Outdoors the yelling and screeching started up again. It had been going on all day. The poor quality public announcement system was calling the Muslim men to prayer on every street corner. It had been calling them since five in the morning. I covered my ears. "How long are they going to keep that up?"

"One month," she said. "And when the month is over we'll have a big feast and get presents. Like Christmas. They're both religious holidays."

"That's a long time to go without sleep. How are these jeans?" I looked at my thighs, which seemed magnified ten times in the mirror. At five foot eight inches and a hundred and twenty pounds, I was the shortest and fattest in my family—a fact my mother never tired of reminding me of.

"You look good in them," Frana said, then sighed. "I can't wait until six so I can eat."

"Why wait?"

"I'm fasting. I can't eat when the sun's up," she said.

"But you don't need to lose weight like I do," I said.

"It's Ramadan, not a diet."

"I don't understand your religion, going hungry, and wearing those tents if you're a woman."

"We don't have to wear them. The Quran only says we have to be modest. You can interpret that any way you like. Isn't it the same with Christianity? Don't different groups interpret your Bible in different ways?"

"Yes, but everyone agrees the Bible is the word of God told by the disciples of Jesus."

"No, not everyone. The Quran is the word of God told directly to the Prophet Muhammad by the angel Gabriel."

"All right, let's drop it. There's enough blood shed over religion and I just had my sheets washed."

* * *

The embassy theater was a circular brick one-story building connected to the three-story embassy. It cost a dollar to get in and fifty cents for popcorn in a plastic Glad sandwich bag. Marines sporting navy blue USMC sweatshirts sold the tickets. When I bought my ticket I recognized the red-haired Marine. But I forgot his name. Unfortunately, he remembered mine. "Ronni-I-gotta-go, how are you?" he asked. I smiled, bought my ticket, and left. What was his name, Red? No, Rocky or something.

As we waited by the double glass doors and Luke bought popcorn, a cranky VW bug rattled by and turned into the parking lot. Two boys slid out through the windows, high-fived each other, and strode across the lawn towards us. I heard Frana catch her breath. "It's Shawnee. He must be home from Oxford." She pointed at the one on the left, a dark-haired guy with thick brows that met over serious eyes set deep in walnut-colored skin.

Ah, I thought; so that was the reason Frana wanted to go to Oxford.

"His father's the prime minister." She bounced on her toes, and then gripped my hand as if to keep from floating away. "He was a senior two years ago when I was in the eighth grade. Isn't he cute?"

"Yes," I agreed, not meaning it because he wasn't my type. However, the guy on the right was wicked adorable. He had hair the reddish brown of fox fur, eyes that flickered with life and a grin that radiated through the space that separated us and sizzled down my spine like a lightening bolt. "Who's that?" I asked when I could find my breath.

"Oh, that's Matt East," Frana said in the kind of bored voice my mom used whenever she asked about my grades.

"Matt East," I repeated, trying the name out on my lips as I fluffed my hair. It would be so cool if Shawnee stopped to talk to Frana and Matt noticed me and . . . A horrible thought shattered my daydream. "Is Matt any relationship to—?"

"He's Danny's brother," Frana confirmed. "But he's nothing like Danny."

Not that anyone would want to be, I thought. Danny East—the annoying class clown. He didn't realize no one liked him, so he always tagged along.

A chill slithered down my spine. Who was I kidding? I wasn't thin enough or pretty enough. Matt would take one look at my braces and pimples and run. Matt walked with an easy grace, as if he'd never had a doubt or defeat in his whole life. Why would someone like him be interested in me?

"I don't think they're meeting anyone," Frana whispered as the boys bought their tickets. "Come on, let's bump into them—by accident. Then I'll talk to Shawnee and you talk to Matt."

"But I came with Luke," I argued. "What will he think?"

Frana patted her bangs. "Half an hour ago you said this wasn't a date, you were just going to the movies together. So why do you care what he thinks?"

I glanced at the popcorn line and saw that Luke would be a few more minutes. Frana had a point. It wasn't like his mom drove me to the theater, and it wasn't like he bought my ticket or offered to buy a drink with the popcorn, which was only fifty cents a bag. Besides he'd been copying my homework for two weeks, so he owed me. Maybe that was the only reason he asked me.

I felt tears sting the edges of my eyes. Lately it seemed I didn't matter to anyone besides Frana. Shawn had dumped me, Mom preferred Amy, and Dad had no time for anything except his job. Frana was the only one who knew me inside and out; she told me I was pretty, my braces weren't hideous, and assured me of my intelligence and loyalty as a friend.

I bit my lip as Shawnee and Matt collected their tickets and turned towards the refreshment stand. If someone like Matt cared about me, then I would be important. I'd have a place. But he couldn't care about me unless he got to know me, and he couldn't get to know me unless he noticed me.

"Okay," I said. "Let's go." I moved towards the boys, towing Frana along.

"Not yet," she hissed. "I have to check my hair." It hung in the long braid she always wore so I didn't know how it could get messed up but I waited while she withdrew a comb and mirror from her purse.

I took the mirror when she finished and looked at my face. Another bump had emerged on my chin. "I can't, my skin."

Frana peered at me. "I don't see anything. But, if it bothers you, why don't you put on some makeup?" She never wore any because her skin was a perfect clear bronze.

"I'm not allowed to wear any. Mom says I'm too young." Another of her stupid rules, I thought. Matt was in college, he'd never notice a girl whose lips didn't glow with pink lipstick. I glanced at Matt and Shawnee parked at the end of the line. "Let's forget the whole idea."

Frana slipped the mirror into her purse. "No. I want to talk to Shawnee, and I'm not going over there alone." She threaded her arm through mine and yanked me along. "Let's get a Coke before the movie starts," she said.

Okay, maybe my zit wasn't so bad, and I could always keep my mouth shut. Maybe it would work. "Good idea," I said, not sure it was.

"Do you have any money?"

"Yes," I said as we closed in on the boys. "I'll get it out of my purse."

I opened my purse with my free hand and began to dig through it. The strap slipped from my shoulder. The purse gaped open. A tampon flew out. I broke away from Frana and dove for it just as Frana said, "Hello," and the boys turned around.

The tampon landed between Matt's feet. I snatched it as Frana extended her hand to Shawnee. "Hi, I remember you from school."

I looked up as Matt loomed over me. I grimaced. *What an idiot.* I awkwardly got off the floor and stood stupidly brushing myself off. Okay now, I was a klutz with braces and a bad complexion. I'm sure Matt would never forget me.

"Shawnee, this is my friend Ronni, and, Ronni, this is Matt," Frana said, in the way of introductions.

Over Matt's shoulder, I saw Luke holding the three bags of popcorn, his eyes nearly closed in a squint.

I waved at him, eager to escape. "I'm sorry. We have to go." I stammered. "Our friend's waiting."

Matt nodded. "Nice to meet y'all."

Frana reached over and shook Shawnee's hand. "Nice to run into you again."

During the movie, I sat between Frana and Luke and held the popcorn on my lap. Its burnt smell clashed with Luke's Old Spice aftershave. After a while his callused hand brushed mine and awkwardly held it. At the same time, Frana whispered in my ear, "Poor Shawnee, his father's in jail. General Zia says he rigged the elections." But my mind was several seats back, and the whole time I had to fight off the urge to turn around and see where Matt sat.

After the movie we stood on the curb. Luke leaned in and asked, "Ronni, you know there's this winter dance and, well, if you aren't going with anyone else, maybe we could go?"

Out of the corner of my eye, I watched Matt and Shawnee cross the embassy lawn and disappear. "What?"

"The Winter dance?" he whispered. "Do you want to go?"

"Sure. That would be good," I agreed resigned. Matt would never ask me to the dance.

Before my mom arrived, Luke leaned over and put his open mouth on mine. I moved back, startled. *Wow, he kissed me.* Embarrassed, I moved in and quickly touched his lips with mine so he wouldn't feel bad.

The awkward moment after the kiss ended when my mom blasted the car horn. I rushed into the car before Frana, avoiding Luke's eyes. As we drove away, I turned to Frana and whispered, "Did you see that? He kissed me."

"And?" she asked.

"It was weird. He asked me to the dance."

"It's not for two months. Are you going?"

"Yeah, I guess," I answered.

Maybe when I flowed gracefully onto the dance floor, Matt would notice how beautiful I looked in my dress and ask me to dance with him. It would be like Cinderella and Prince Charming.

Chapter Eight

I entered Mom's studio and found her sketching a Pakistani girl from a photo. "Mom, I need to order a dress for the winter dance. Do you have the newest Sears Catalog?"

Mom turned around and stared at me. "You were asked to the dance? We don't need the catalog. I have some fashion magazines in the living room. I can get the tailor to make you one. Ask Rashid to come in here."

I didn't have to call; when I turned around Rashid stood at the edge of the wooden screen blocking off the room. He was like Casper the Ghost slipping through walls unexpectedly. "Memsahib, need help?"

"Yes," Mom said. "Could you ask the man who sews the clothes how he's doing on the list I gave him?"

"The Durzi," Rashid said. I nodded. He'd already taught me the word for tailor.

"Yes. And Rashid, I need you to help me with a sketch. I can't get the hands right on this picture. I need you to sit for me and let me sketch your hands and face. I have a headdress for you to wear like the girl's. It will only be for a few hours."

"You want him to dress like a girl so you can sketch him?" I asked.

"Ronni, stay out of it," she said, handing Rashid the colored scarf for his head. Rashid's eyes widened and he looked as though she held out a poisonous snake for him to take.

Instead of taking the cloth, Rashid backpedaled out of the room. "I tell the Durzi," he said as he fled.

"Wait," she called, looking confused at the cloth.

I hadn't asked Mom to have any clothes made for me, but she had ordered some anyway. "You're so lucky," she said. "When I was little, my mom was a great seamstress. But when I asked her to sew something special for me she wouldn't."

I'd heard the story before, so I yawned and nodded, "Uhnhm."

"In fact, when I was sixteen I won a contest in *Seventeen* magazine. Because of my artistic talent, I drew the perfect outfit, but your grandmother refused to make it for me, so I lost the prize."

"That's great, Mom." I said, wanting to get past the old news. "But most kids wear Levis and stuff with tags from expensive stores. Couldn't we get my dress from the catalog?"

Mom glared at me. "You're so ungrateful, Ronni."

I'd hurt her feelings. Groaning inside, I gave in. I would get a new dress sewn for the dance. All I had to do was find the picture of something I wanted.

A week later, Frana helped me pick something out. We lay on our stomachs on the living room floor with our long legs bent at the knees. Fashion magazines cluttered the floor. I spotted a long V-necked dress in pink with capped sleeves.

"What do you think of this one, only in green?" I slid the book over.

"It's nice. It would pick up the green in your eyes," she said. "I got mine shipped from Tehran. It's orange. And I'm going to braid my hair with silver thread. I'll curl yours for you."

"Thanks." I slid the magazine back and turned down the corner. "Orange'd look great on you. I can't believe you had the nerve to call up Shawnee and ask him." I'd never have that much nerve.

She grinned. "We talked for a long time."

Rashid walked in and glanced at the magazines opened in front of us. His face scrunched up, but before he could say anything, Mom called, "Rashid, I need your help with this sketch. Rashid, where are you?"

I giggled as Rashid darted behind the curtains. "Mom wants him to dress like a girl so she can finish a sketch," I told Frana. Then I asked. "Do you think Luke's cute?" I knew there was no way Luke could compare to Matt, but I thought he was cute, and I hoped no one would consider me a complete fool for going to the dance with him.

"He's okay. Not as cute as Shawnee, though." She grinned. "But we can't all be so lucky."

She picked up a magazine to return it to me, and a piece of notebook paper fell out. "What's this?" she asked, studying the repeated words. "Mrs. Veronica East. Did you write this?"

I grabbed for it, but she held it out of my reach, sat up and turned her back on me. "How many times did you write it?" she asked flipping it over. "A hundred?"

I lunged around her and snatched it, feeling my face grow hot as the blood rushed in. In fact, I thought about Matt all the time: what it would be like to kiss him, how his arms would feel around me. I wondered if he'd want to sleep with me. I'd never had sex, but I was sure he had, being in college and all. How many times had I looked at the half heart in my jewelry box and dreamed that he had one that fit mine. "It was one of my more hopeful moments." I folded the paper.

"Hopefully in love, you mean," Frana said. "You just met him and you're dating Luke."

"Stop it. I like Luke. I'm going to the dance with Luke. Some of us aren't lucky in love, Mrs. Frana Bhutto. Or is it Mrs. Prime Mistress?"

"You're so silly. He's not the next in line for power. Being prime minister isn't like being the shah or king. Besides, he's the youngest. He has an older brother."

Just then Amy walked in. I slipped my list of Veronica Easts into my geography notebook.

"What are you doing?" She circled around us, peering at the magazines.

I slammed them shut and glared at her. "None of your business."

"If you get a new dress, Mom has to get the tailor to make me one, too." She turned toward the kitchen to yell, "Mom. Mom!" What a freaking baby, always sticking her nose into my business.

*   *   *

Mom drove me to the local bazaar to find fabric. Dozens of individual shops lined the narrow asphalt street. Some of the shops were shaded by tin awnings that hung from the front of plaster buildings. Others baked in full sunlight. Wares from food to fabric spilled from big burlap sacks, straw baskets, blankets spread on the street, or rickety wooden crates.

There were no rows of labeled, prepackaged, FDA approved chips or doughnuts beckoning from orderly white shelves. Squawking chickens trampled each other in cramped pens stacked sky high. As we passed one stand, the youthful mustached vendor followed us, holding a squealing chicken upside down by its gnarled legs. "Memsahib," he called, "you buy. Berry fresh." Mom darted by other shoppers, leaving me to fend for myself.

I ducked my head. Where the hell was Mom? *Get me out of here.* "No, thank you," I whispered.

The man kept up with me. "I kill, you see."

What? Was he telling me he would kill me if I didn't buy his stupid chicken? I sped up, scanning the area for my mom, but the vendor hung at my elbow. When I glanced back at him, he swung his chicken toward me. "What are you talking about? What are you going to kill?"

He ran in front of me and blocked my way. "For you." He made a motion like cracking the chicken's neck. I guarded my own neck in shock. *He'd break the chicken's neck, right in front of me. Eww!* "No, thanks. I like Foster Farms, twelve drumsticks. No feathers or eyes."

He stared blankly and shook the chicken at me. "I clean berry nice, Memsahib."

I bolted from the chicken salesman and ran to catch up with my mom. I darted past vegetable shops, where fruit sat out in the open without plastic wrap to keep out insects. Red weevils danced in the flour, while bees stole the nectar from seeping fruit and flies laid eggs in spices. Gray-haired men puffed on long pipes and the smoke swirled around in the air, blending with the smells of dried red peppers, curry, mint leaves, dye from bolts of fabric, and the foul water in stagnant black and green puddles nearby.

Some shops had buyers negotiating the price of wares measured by the length of a merchant's arm or by the weight calculated in the palm of a hand. Shoppers paid in rupees, and purchases were wrapped in day-old newspaper. People thrust twisted wood cravings and bruised oranges in my face, calling to me, "Memsahib, you like. You buy. Berry good." I hurried on.

Mom had stopped before the fabric shop and held up turquoise-colored fabric. "This will match your eyes better than the green." As she touched the bolt of material, the merchant rushed over to unfold it for her, "Memsahib, you like, you buy."

"Will it shrink?"

"No, berry good. You buy little money. Ten rupees." The little vendor unfolded more of the fabric and measured it from his index finger to his chin.

Mom said, "Okay, I'll take seven yards." She held up seven fingers. He smiled and cut the fabric with what looked like old rusty garden sheers, and then he folded it and wrapped it in newspaper.

What would Matt think when he saw me in the dress?

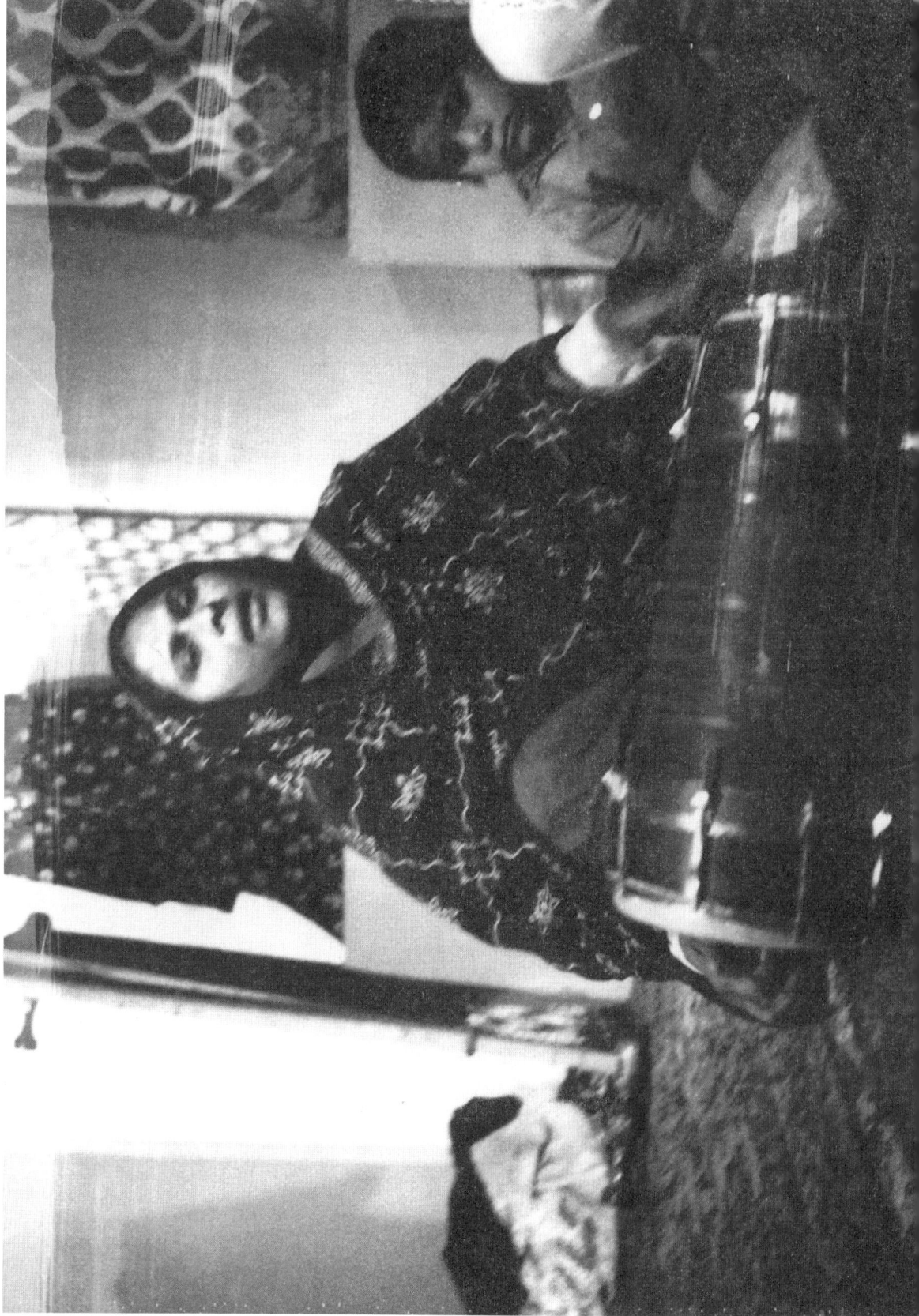

Chapter Nine

A week later, Luke stopped me at my locker. "Did you finish the map for history?" he smiled his cocky smile.

"Yeah, I did it the night it was assigned. Why?" I asked. "You didn't?"

"Can I use yours?" he pleaded. "Ple...ease, come on, you always get an A."

"Mine isn't going to help you on the test." Everyday Luke sat across from me on the bus. During the ride his Converse tennis shoe would kick mine "accidentally" and every morning he'd ask to see my homework. He was unofficially my boyfriend, a stand-in for the real thing, because I wasn't sure I'd ever have a real boyfriend again.

Using my most nasal, authoritative voice, and imitating our history teacher, Mrs. Cook, I said, "Pakistan is the shape of a duck with two pair of legs. Each pair of legs touches the warm water of the Arabian Sea to the south. Its tail is against Iran in the southwest and its back curves around Afghanistan to the west. The bill of the duck pokes into China in the northeast, while it pushes out its chest into India in the east."

"Very funny, Ronni. Come on, let me see the map." He winked and gently placed his hand on my hip. Warmth flowed through me and for a moment I imagined I belonged with him. I belonged somewhere.

I watched his lips, wanting to kiss his soft full mouth, but I knew too many eyes looked on for that.

"What's in it for me?" I teased.

He pinned my left shoulder against the locker. "I won't let you go until you give it to me." *He wanted me and he needed me.*

"Okay, okay." He let me go to dig into my locker, and I lifted up my geography notebook to hand to him.

As he reached for it, a piece of notebook paper fell out. My Veronica East scribbling. Oh, *no.* I dove to grab the paper back. He retrieved it and looked at it. His smile became a scowl. "What is this, Mrs. Veronica East? Ronni?"

I snatched it back and kept my eyes on the floor. What could I say? I was caught. I couldn't think.

He grabbed my hand. "What? Why do you have this, Ronni?"

My brain began to work. "Uhm, it's . . . it's. Well, Frana wrote it as a, well, a joke. It's nothing really."

I sounded stupid, and he must have seen through the lie because he twisted my wrist. It burned.

"Stop, Luke, that hurts." I pulled back my hand and rubbed it.

"You like Danny, don't you?"

"What?" He thought I liked Matt's silly brother. "No. No way."

He shoved me against locker. The combination lock bit into my back. "Ahh! Stop, that hurts."

"Forget it." He walked away, but turned back after a few steps. "And you kiss like a fish." *I did what? What did he mean I kissed like a fish? How dare he say that!*

A few people walked by. Bowing my head to avoid their stares, I started after him. "Wait!" I called.

He turned, shoved me against another locker, and yelled, "Forget the dance, too."

I sagged against the locker; my book and papers fell from my hand. I got up as quickly as I could and glanced around me. *Everyone had seen. They'd all know. What would they say? Did they see him shove me? Act natural, like nothing happened. So, he didn't want to go to the dance anymore. I couldn't go; Matt wouldn't see me in my dress. I wouldn't be Cinderella and there'd be no Prince Charming.*

Ian stopped, picked up my book, and put my papers in it. "Ronni, you okay?"

"It's nothing. I'm fine," I sniffed.

No dance! What was I going to do? Who had seen our fight? I brushed the hair out of my eyes and glanced around to see if anyone laughed at me. A few people stared. I met their gazes and they quickly looked away. Rising, I snatched the book from Ian without glancing up at him or saying thank you and took off to find Frana.

I found her in the bathroom. "Frana," I gasped.

"What's wrong with you? You're red."

"Luke broke up with me. We aren't going to the dance. He found the stupid paper with Veronica East all over it. Why didn't I throw it away? I'm so stupid."

Frana and I looked at each other over the mirror in the sink. "So, what now?" Frana asked.

"I don't know. Everyone will be at the dance and they'll all know. Luke and I didn't go because . . . What will he say happened?"

Frana put her arm around me. "Slow down. It'll be okay."

I gasped for air and continued, "Will he tell everyone? I'll be a laughingstock. He's really mad. And what if he tells Danny and Danny tells Matt? He'll think I'm stupid." I shook my head at her.

Frana smiled at me and patted my back. "It'll be okay. You're not a laughingstock. Do you like Luke?"

"I . . . I don't know. I like Matt. But he isn't here most of the time and he doesn't know I exist. Why should he?"

Frana waved that aside and persisted, "Do you like Luke?"

"I heard you. He likes me. Most girls would die to have him like them. Wouldn't they?"

"But do you like him?'

I swirled to face her. "What are you, my psychiatrist? He's okay. I want to go to the dance and he likes me. Or he did. You know how it is, everyone looking at you, knowing your business. You get close to someone and you have to leave them because your parents get transferred to a different place." I shook my head and looked into the mirror at my red eyes. "And your parents. They laugh and say, 'How cute, puppy love, their little crush. Oh, you'll find someone else, say goodbye.' And you leave and it's like nothing ever happened." Frana returned her hand to my back. "It wasn't important. You don't matter." I added more softly, "It'd be nice to matter."

"You matter." She brushed back a strand of my hair. "You have to matter to you before you can matter to anyone else."

I brushed away a tear, "No, I don't matter, not even to my mom. I wanted to go to the dance with you and Shawnee. We were going to have fun, right? But now what?" I asked.

She looked at her watch.

"I know we're late. I'm sorry." I grabbed her hand and squeezed it. Our friendship bracelets clinked together. We'd always be friends. I'd never have a better one.

"No problem. Let's go."

*   *   *

I knew I had to tell Mom. She'd offered to drive us to the dance. And what about the dress? What would I say if she said something stupid, like, "There'll be other dances" or "If you only stood up straighter, none of this would have happened?" I had to act like I didn't care. Like this was no big deal. I found her in her studio working on a red pastel of a horse and rider. "Mom, did the tailor already finish my dress for the dance next week?"

"Yes, today," she said brightly. "It's in my bedroom. Want to try it on?"

"No, I'm not going."

That got her to look up from her sketch, "Why not?"

"Luke... we had a fight today, and we aren't going out anymore."

She shrugged. "Well, there are other boys, aren't there? What about that East boy?"

How did she know about Matt? "What? Who?"

"Danny East?" she asked. "I play bridge with his mother. Why don't you go with him?"

"Danny! No way." Could it get any worse? My mom wanted to fix me up with the wrong son of her friend. "I'm not going with Danny. Everyone would laugh at me." And what would Matt think? If I dated his little brother he'd think I was a stupid kid.

Rashid entered the room. "Memsahibs, dinner ready."

"Okay, Rashid. I still need your help with the sketch, so don't desert me tomorrow."

"Yes, Memsahib," he said looking frightened. Poor kid. I knew how he felt being controlled by my mom.

"Mom, I can sit for the sketch."

"No, you're not small enough. I need someone with delicate features. If you were thinner maybe."

I swallowed the insult like another bitter lump and said, "I don't think Rashid wants to be sketched as a girl."

"He doesn't mind."

If I argued with her, she'd just get angry with me. "What are you going to do with the dress for the dance?" I asked, changing the subject.

"Nothing. You can wear the dress another time. Go get ready for dinner."

*   *   *

Two nights later, we gathered at the dinner table as usual. Our cook, Akbar, always baked fresh bread for Wednesday nights. I tried not to think about the weevils he had to sift out of the flour and concentrate on how great it was. The bearer, Mohammed, always served us at a long oak table set with cloth place mats, and Rashid poured the water. Mom insisted that all the napkins, dinner, and salad plates matched.

After Rashid filled Amy's water glass and retreated, Dad turned to Mom and asked, "Did you hear that Sergeant Elvis's son is sick with dysentery? He drank some water that hadn't been boiled and filtered." He turned his gaze on me. "Didn't you baby-sit for him, Ronni?"

"Yeah," I said between bites of the warm, soft center of the homemade bread.

"You didn't drink any water. Did you?" he asked.

I didn't answer right away because I was busy chewing.

Amy cut in, "Mom, since Ronni isn't going to the Winter Dance, can I use the dress the tailor made for her?" She gave me a stupid sly look. "Luke asked me. I told him I could go, and now I need a dress."

The bread became a rock stuck in my throat. I choked. Amy smiled at me the way a cat smiles at a mouse. I coughed up the bread.

Mom glared at me. "Ronni, slow down. You always eat too fast. And sit up straight." I wished I could yell, "shut up," to her and punch Amy in her big ugly mouth.

"Mom, can I?" Amy asked again, her eyes on me, "Huh? Can I?"

"Sure, honey, I'll give you a ride."

Suddenly, I didn't want to eat. But it was a family rule that I couldn't excuse myself until my plate was empty. So I forked the tasteless grub into my mouth, chewed, and swallowed.

The whole time Amy chatted stupidly with Mom about her silly dance plans. I wanted to run, to hide, to cry, and to scream. How could she go with him? She sat like a snake, her eyes darting from Mom to me, tongue lashing out and whipping me around so my insides ached.

If only I could slap that stupid smile off her face. He pushed me and then he asked her. She, my own sister, said yes and she was going in my dress, my dress. I couldn't breathe. Mom offered her a ride on my date. Mom didn't care.

I wouldn't give her the satisfaction of crying. I waited until I closed the door of my room and sobbed as I wrote in my diary, pouring out all the pages of hurt.

      *   *   *

On the afternoon of the dance, while Amy was getting dressed, Mom yelled, "Ronni!"

"What! What now?" I yelled through the closed door to my bedroom.

"Why do you always get so defensive? I don't even want to call you. Phone."

I stomped downstairs, wondering who it could be.

"Ronni, oh Ronni," Frana said into the phone, "Shawnee's under house arrest."

"What? What'd he do?"

"Nothing. He didn't do anything. It's just that. It's just because they're afraid of him now that his father is being sentenced. They think he'll stir up trouble."

"Wow, wait a minute. Is he okay?" I couldn't imagine being arrested because of who your father was. "Come over. We'll be wallflowers together."

"No, I want to wait by the phone."

"I can come over there." *We'd sit and wait to make sure Shawnee was okay.*

"No. I think I'd rather sit and cry and wait knowing I can call you if I need you."

I summed up in a poem that night, the night I missed the Winter Ball.

> *It was 7:00 on Saturday night. The light illuminated the front steps of our house number 24, at the end of Nara Lane. I stared at the door from my perch at the bend of the stairs, on the night of the Winter Ball.*
>
> *The doorbell rang. Amy answered the chime. Dressed in the turquoise gown made to match my eyes. At the door, dressed in a black suit, a corsage in his hand stood Luke, my ex-boyfriend. On the night of the Winter Ball.*

I rested my head on the rail. If he'd come up the stairs, take my hand, and kneel down as he spoke, he would tell me he was wrong and how sorry he was. He would pin the corsage on me and we'd walk down the stairs. On the night of the Winter Ball.

But Mom appeared with the camera. He pinned the orchid on my sister. They smiled close together, both said, "Cheese." The picture taken, they slipped out the door. So I stayed home on the night of the Winter Ball.

The door to my dad's study hung open and I rapped on the doorframe. He'd been preoccupied and working alone in his study most nights. "What?" He lowered his reading glasses.

"Did you know that Shawnee Bhutto is under house arrest?" I asked, walking in the office. I saw a notepad on which my dad had written, "A.Q. Khan" and "nuclear missiles."

"Yes. His father is still in prison." He reached for his notes and took them from the table.

"Does Pakistan have nuclear weapons?" I asked.

"It's nothing to concern yourself with, Ronni," he said in a tired tone.

"I can't help thinking about Afghanistan and Frana said there is some trouble in Iran with the Shah being sick. Do we have to worry about our safety here, too?"

"No," he said staring down at his Time magazine, avoiding my eyes.

Chapter Ten

When Christmas vacation ended and school resumed, Matt left for the States. Frana said I should forget about him. "Ronni, how about Ian? I think he likes you."

"Really?" I considered the idea briefly. *Ian always knew what to say. If he really got to know me he'd figure out I wasn't cool, that I was too fat, and soon my braces would start to bother him. He wouldn't like me for long.* "He's cool but he hangs out with the stoners, and last week I saw him talking to Katie. I think he's just nice to everyone." *Besides, who could compete with Katie?*

"I don't think you like yourself much."

The next day, Saturday, January 13, Frana and her mom drove Mom and me to Kosher Market. Frana's mom, Fatima, said that they had the freshest meat and they wouldn't fleece Mom on the price. Unfortunately, Amy came along.

The adults sat up front while we occupied the back seat. I wanted a car for my sixteenth birthday, but knew that would never happen. So for the benefit of my mother, I complained, "Happy sixteen. If I were in the States I'd have my driver's license."

"Well, you're not." My mom hadn't even bothered to take her eyes off Fatima, whom she sketched.

The black Lincoln we rode in turned onto Grand Trunk Road and passed block after block of gutted vehicles. All the cars were so naked and rusted their makes and models were unidentifiable. Any part that could be used as a roof, seat, or water container had long been stripped.

A little boy, in nothing more than a t-shirt, and an older boy clutching each other's hands scrounged around the vehicles as though looking for one last piece of metal they could salvage.

"You know, Mom," I joked. "I could get one of these cars and you could pay to fix it up. I'm not asking for much."

A frown of deep concentration hardened on her face and she clutched her pencil shading in an area of her sketch below Fatima's hand. "Ronni, you can't drive until you're eighteen, and that's the end of it." The tip of her pencil broke.

Amy smiled, "When I turn sixteen, Mom's going to buy me a Mustang."

"Not if I run you over first," I muttered.

Amy leaned over the seat. "Did you hear her, Mom?"

Before Mom could answer, we became aware of a noisy mob ahead. I rolled down my window to hear. Voices called, "Allah Muharram! Kalimah! Alaihis-salam. Ayetal Kursi!" ahead of us.

"What's going on up there?" I asked.

The crowd gathered, six or seven rows thick, and the front line of men swung heavy chains with nails or small knives attached to them. The chains struck them across their chests and backs.

"Are they prisoners?" I asked. "Are they dangerous?"

"No, no," Fatima said. "It's Muharram. They're Shiites. ..."

"She who?" Amy asked.

"Shiites. A sect of Muslims. This is a celebration to commemorate the death of our prophet Muhammad's grandson Hussein."

We had studied Shiites and Sunnis, two groups of Muslims, in political science. The groups were like Republicans and Democrats, arguing about who should be the rightful leader, but the Shiites and Sunni's disagreed over religious leadership. People got killed over their religious differences. The funeral was another reminder of how Islam was more than just a religion; religion ruled a Muslim's life. In class, we'd learned they had to pray several times a day and couldn't eat pork or drink alcohol.

With faces plastered against opposite windows, Amy and I stared at the men who struck themselves over and over again. Blood poured out of open wounds on their chests and their faces were sweaty and intense. Trance-like, their dark eyes glassed over as they shouted and bled. A man ground a link of a chain into a bloody sore he had created on his back. The sight made me want to vomit.

"Hussein died over a thousand years ago." Frana spoke frankly.

"What?" I asked, sure this couldn't be any sort of celebration. "This isn't a funeral? They do this every year?"

"Hussein was a martyr," Fatima explained. "He was betrayed and killed defending the true values of Islam. We Shiites believe only through their own suffering can they honor him."

"They're hurting themselves." I grimaced. The car moved along slowly, parting the sea of pained faces. I spun to face Frana. "You don't do that," I whispered. "Do you?"

"No, I'm a woman. But Muharram is still a holy day for all Muslims. We just celebrate it differently. I gave up food today to honor Imam Hussein."

I couldn't imagine not eating all day. I looked outside. The faces offered intense, unwavering faith. Faith so strong it was paid for in shouts, pain, sweat, and blood.

My parents were Unitarians, and because they had yet to find a Unitarian church abroad, they had an excuse to sleep in on Sunday mornings. But, when I got a ride to Sunday school with a neighbor, I developed fond memories of church. I used to sing, "He made the lame to walk and the blind to see," and "Jesus loves the little children ...black and yellow, red and white, they are precious in his sight." Those words gave me comfort. Jesus loved all of us, even the children with fly-caked eyes and twisted limbs.

Sunday school had meant graham crackers and cherry Kool-Aid. I remembered making a tissue paper cross: blue, red, yellow, and green—the colors of the rainbow. A cross Mom claimed was beautiful and dumped in the garbage when my back was turned. As the memory turned sour, I looked back out the car window. My faith didn't draw blood, didn't leave scars. My faith didn't cut too deep. Maybe I would never care about anything so much; the thought saddened me.

Mom asked Fatima to slow down. "I want to sketch this. I need to take some pictures. Is my camera back there, girls?"

Fatima frowned, "It is not really permitted to take pictures of a religious ceremony."

"I'll be very discreet." Mom put her finger to her lips.

I looked at Frana, who gave me a tight-lipped smile. "Mom!" I yelled, "You're sick. You turn everything into a freak show."

Amy, the good daughter, handed her the Polaroid and she started snapping pictures.

"I can't believe you," I complained. "Don't miss any blood."

* * *

The next day after school Frana came over to do homework. "How's Shawnee?" I asked.

"He is still under house arrest, but he sounded okay. I just hope they stop messing with him."

"Why doesn't he go back to Oxford?"

"His father is still in prison and he could be sentenced any day. Shawnee wants to be close for his father."

"Okay, I guess we have to get back to these boring reports," I shuffled my papers and handed one to Frana, who sat across from me on my bed.

Mrs. Cook had assigned yet another biographical report on a political figure of our choice. "I'm sick of stupid reports that start out, "he was born April 19, 1872, et cetera, et cetera." Can't we ever do anything interesting?" I threw my notes across the room.

"We have the highest grades in the class. I'm sure we can make our reports interesting."

I stared at her for a moment. Maybe she had a point. "You're right." We could do something different. We could make it fun. "How about we chose a controversial person? Maybe two who hate each other? Then you and I can make a presentation taking on the personalities of our characters and give opposing sides of an argument. We can even dress up like our characters." I shuddered, imagining being made fun of for dressing up, but it might help maintain our edge.

"Hey, that's not bad. How about Muhammad Reza Shah and the Ayatollah Khomeini? They despise one another. I'll present the Shah's side while you can take the Ayatollah. What do you say?"

In World History, Mrs. Cook had us read about the problems in Iran. Apparently the Shah Muhammad Reza Shah was like the king. He kicked out the religious fanatic, the Ayatollah Khomeini for bad-mouthing him. Anyway, now that the Shah had cancer, the Ayatollah's popularity increased. I could write a good argument. "Yeah okay, but let's not do the 'he was born on a dark and stormy night' junk. I'll argue the Ayatollah's point of view, like a debate and you take the Shah's. That way you can argue that the monarchy has been in power these many years and that will give some background information without sounding boring. You think Cook'll let us do that?"

A light knock sounded at my door. "Who's there?" I asked.

"Rashid," he whispered.

I grumbled as I uncrossed my legs and went to open the door. He hurried in, glancing behind him as though he were being chased.

"What's wrong?"

"Memsahib, looks me. She wants make picture of me." His eyes darted about the room.

I laughed. "Just make her happy and let her draw you or else she'll never leave you alone. Believe me, I know," I told him. I had had to sit for my mother numerous times. I even had a scar from a time I didn't want to sit and she grabbed my wrist. Her fingernail jabbed me and left a mark.

"No, Allah not like this." Rashid shook his head so hard I thought it might fling off.

"Allah doesn't like your picture drawn?" I frowned and looked to Frana for some clarification but she just smiled. "Why?"

"Allah not like," he repeated glancing at the door again as though it might open any minute.

"Some illiterate people believe that if they have their picture taken or drawn they lose a piece of their soul," Frana explained. "He doesn't want his soul trapped in your mom's sketch pad."

"Wow. Then I'm in real trouble. My soul is scattered in a dozen sketch pads and a few pastels around the house."

"Allah be mad," Rashid repeated, wrapping his skinny arms around himself.

"Okay. You can hide in here," I told him. "But, we're doing homework, so you have to be quiet."

Rashid went over to the side of the bed farthest from the door and sat on the floor cross-legged.

Frana smiled at him and then continued talking about the report. "I can start by telling everyone why I sent you into exile, and you can defend yourself."

"Okay. So..." I took out my notes on Iran. "I'm the Ayatollah, a fundamentalist Shiite Muslim, and I'm opposed to your policy of letting government officials be sworn in on whatever Holy Scripture they choose."

"Shiite no good," Rashid said popping his head up.

"We're talking about the Ayatollah," I told him. "But Shiites are Muslims too, so why are they bad?"

Rashid lowered his head again. "Not good," he mumbled.

"I'm a Shiite," Frana said.

Rashid popped his head up over the bedspread again. "You no good."

He disappeared as I said, "Rashid, that's rude. Frana's okay. You like her."

He rose up to shake his head and vanish again. "No good."

"Rashid, we have homework. So if you want to stay, you can't insult Frana."

He peered around the side of the bed "Okay, Runny." Then he muttered something about the Shiites under his breath and moved farther away from Frana.

I ignored him. "You banished me because I stirred up trouble," I said to Frana. "I also object to your father's banning of the veil in 1936 and your westernization of the country—"

My door swung open and slammed off the back wall. Rashid dove under the bed. I spun to see my sister in the doorway.

"Did you steal my tennis shoes?" she asked. "I can't find them. They were in my room yesterday."

"Get out of here." I jumped up and blocked her from entering my room. "What do I want with your stinking shoes?"

"Maybe because you're jealous that I'm trying out for basketball, and you can't make the team." How did she know what I could or couldn't do? Stupid crybaby.

"We're busy. Leave." I pushed her out the door.

"Get your hands off me," she yelled. I closed the door on her. "Mom!" I heard outside my door. "I think Ronni stole my shoes, and she won't let me check in her room!"

"I can't stand that little brat," I complained to Frana.

Rashid popped out from behind the bed. "Runny, you want me find Memsahib Amy shoes?"

"No. Let her find her own shoes." Dumb fool, thinking she could bully me. Jealous of her? Get real. I shoved my hair out of my eyes and stared at my notes. "Where were we?"

"I have continued to modernize Iran," Frana said. "Following in my father's, Reza Shah's, footsteps but many Iranians object to my alliance with the United States and—"

My door flew open again, and Mom walked into the room with Amy grinning beside her. "Ronni, do you have Amy's shoes?"

I glared up at her but remained seated. "We're studying. Besides, what do I need her shoes for? Proof that Bigfoot really does exist?"

"Don't get smart with me," Mom said, turning around to leave. She stopped when she saw Rashid. "Rashid, I want you to sit for a picture. I haven't had a chance to sketch you yet."

"I find Memsahib Amy shoe now." Rashid rushed out of the room, sliding by Mom like a slippery little fish.

When the door shut, Frana asked, "Do you want to try out for basketball?"

I dreamed of being on a sports team. They got to travel to India and other places. I had joined the 100-mile running club, and I did pretty well. But the club was all about individual effort. It involved keeping a personal record of miles run. I wasn't the fastest, so I had to run the most, and for that I got a certificate. Yet anything that involved teamwork snared me. I didn't perform well under pressure.

My mom often told a joke at dinner parties about what a great athlete I was. It went like this, "Ronni won third place in the 100-yard relay last year. What we don't tell anyone is that there were only three runners." I wanted more than anything else to be part of a team but not at the expense of being a laughingstock.

"No," I answered Frana. "Let's finish our reports."

"No. Let's practice a few free shots first. You and I are going to make the basketball team and shut your pesty little sister up." *What if I could make the team? Mom would watch from the sidelines and realize how great I was and how she'd been wrong. I really was the better daughter.*

I followed Frana out into the yard to practice dribbling and free shots on the rim that Dad had put up over the garage for Amy. I made a shot and Frana cheered. Frana and I would be the most valuable players. With Frana's help I could finally shine at something.

Chapter Eleven

The next day, Frana didn't come to school. Where was she? I'd have felt completely lost if I hadn't hung around with Ian all day. That afternoon he promised to call. Maybe Frana was right. He liked me. He wasn't gorgeous like Luke, but he was popular. "Why don't we hang out like this more often?" he asked.

"Maybe because of your girlfriends," I said.

"Oh, yeah." He grinned. "Well, how about I dump all other girls and you and I go out?"

My stomach tingled with excitement or fear or maybe both. *Did he just ask me out? If I got too involved would I be able to get out when he threw me over for some other girl?* I had to call Frana when I got home to find out what she thought. "Stop kidding around," I said, and changed the subject.

After school, I walked ahead of Amy, in a rush to get home and call Frana. The smell of peanut butter cookies filled the house and I went into the kitchen to get some before I used the phone. There was a muffled sound of a man's and two women's voices coming from the living room. Did Mom have another victim in the house?

She had a habit of dragging home stray natives to draw. Once she'd brought home a street sweeper with rotten teeth. For four rupees, approximately ten cents, the sweeper happily sat for Mom. The week before, she'd brought home a snake charmer. He played his flute, made out of a yellow gourd, as a diamond-headed cobra quivered from side to side in a hypnotic trance, slowly uncoiling out of its straw basket. After that, I checked under my blanket each night to make sure no poisonous snakes waited to kill me while I slept.

As I headed for the stairs, I stopped beside the living room door and listened to see if I could figure out who was posing for Mom. I was surprised when I heard Frana's voice. When I peeked in, I saw Frana, her mother, father, and little brother. Frana's dad, the ambassador of Iran, had only been to our house for one dinner party. What were they doing? Why hadn't she been in school? Behind me, the door slammed as Amy entered.

Mom turned and spotted me. "Ronni?" She quickly glanced back at Fatima and then her eyes darted to me again, "Take Frana and go up to your room."

"What's going on?" I asked.

"Ronni, just go." Mom cut her eyes at me in a warning and turned away.

As we climbed the steps, Frana brushed against the wall as though she could sink into it.

I didn't say another word until we'd arrived on the second floor. "What's the matter? Are you sick or something? I missed you in school." She averted her eyes and picked at a cuticle on her thumb.

When we got to my room, I glanced toward Amy's on the other side of the hall. But Amy's voice traveled up from the kitchen. I closed and locked the door, sensing that Frana had a secret to divulge.

She paced and ran her finger along the dresser and the edge of my jewelry box. I sat on my bed. "I had to hang around with Ian all day because you weren't there. He asked me out." I waited, but she didn't say anything. "I can't go out with him, can I?"

"Why?" Frana asked without looking at me.

"Well." This wasn't the way I had hoped the conversation would go. Frana seemed distant, but I continued, "We'd go out and he'd get bored with me and then he'd leave. People always leave."

"Ronni, you're the best friend anyone could ask for." She faced me and forced a smile. "I'll miss you."

"What? What are you talking about?" I'll miss you? What was that about? "Are you going somewhere?" I asked.

She turned back to the dresser and started to arrange the lip-gloss, hair clips, brush, and lotions on my dresser. Something was really wrong. I wanted to go to her and tell her everything would be all right but she hadn't told me what troubled her yet. She had always been like the moon, able to live in two separate worlds, illuminating my dark ignorance with her soft light. My moon had suddenly been eclipsed. *Was I in some kind of trouble? I couldn't think of anything I'd done.*

When Frana turned towards me, tears welled up in her eyes. "The Shah fled Iran yesterday."

That was it? So what? Was she worried about how that would affect our group report. Who cared? Someone else would rule the country; it wouldn't affect us. "I'm sorry. Did you know him?"

"No but that's not it, Ronni. We have to leave Pakistan. My parents came here to ask your parents for help. We're going to flee to the U.S."

She was leaving Pakistan? I scooted to the edge of the bed. "What? When? But why?" Then I whispered "Is someone after you?"

"No, but we can't stay. My father no longer represents Iran, and we can't go back home to Iran. They think my father is Savak."

"Savak?"

"Savak, the Shah's secret police. If we go back, my father will have to stand trial. He'll be found guilty even though he's innocent and they'll kill him." She broke down sobbing.

What could I say? She loved her dad. What would I do if they were going to kill my dad? I was as useful to her as a stone, sitting on the bed while she stood weeping.

Finally, I got up and put my arm around her. "I'm sorry. How can my parents help?"

"They'll help us get political asylum in the U.S." She cried harder and we sat down. I rested my arm around her, dead weight pushing on her shoulder.

When her mother called, she reached in her pocket and took out a note. "We can't go home, and I can't call Shawnee. He won't know where I am. He lives at number 70 Clifton Road. Can you get this to him?" She handed me the paper. Frana's life had come to resemble Shawnee's. Both their fathers' lives were in danger. Being an American I was safe; my dad was safe. I pushed away memories of Kabul.

How could I get to 70 Clifton Road? Wasn't that like getting to the White House? Would there be guards? I wanted to ask her if Shawnee was still under house arrest and if I could get arrested, but she had enough to worry about.

"I will," I whispered, as I took the note. "And we'll write every day. Nothing will change. Not between us. When everything's settled, you'll come back. You can't leave, not forever."

"The world is a small place," Frana said.

But as I watched her leave, I thought only of the huge ocean that would divide us.

Chapter Twelve

When Frana left, I went to talk to Mom. "Mom, I need a ride to Prime Minister Bhutto's house."

"What? Where?" She glanced up from the pastel sketch she worked on.

"It's at 70 Clifton Road. I have to go there, tonight."

"No. Why would you want to go there?" Before I could answer, she continued. "I'm in the middle of working here. I have to finish this sketch."

"Fine." I stormed off. People never mattered to her unless they posed for her. I wished I could steal the keys to the jeep, but where was Clifton Road? If I got caught I'd go to jail.

I flung myself on my bed and picked up my diary. I took out thirty dollars. I'd only managed to save ten dollars since I arrived in Pakistan—my get-away money. But now I had nowhere to get away to. I wasn't going to use the money to go home to Morocco; Shawn was just another memory like all the other friends I'd left behind. He'd forgotten me, but Frana wouldn't. I wanted to get Frana something. I couldn't do what I wanted for her, but I'd buy her something to remember me by.

There was a soft tapping on my door. I hid the money under my blanket. "Yes?"

Rashid opened the door and stuck his head in. "You want go to 70 Clifton Road? I take you."

"How? You don't have a car."

"We take bus," he said.

I pictured the crowded, dirty lopsided buses with people crammed body to body. I'd probably get attacked. I was a girl; it was dangerous. "I can't take the bus."

"Yes. You have rupees? You need the burka. You wear. I take you," he said.

My mom had a burka or sheet-like dress that covered her from head to toe. "Okay, Rashid, I need you to buy something for me." I produced the thirty dollars. "I need you to help me buy a gift for Frana. It needs to be good. I want to get her a silver Fatima's hand, a real silver one from the market." I thought it was the best idea I ever had. Frana's mom was Fatima, named after Fatima, the Islamic Prophet Muhammad's daughter. A Fatima's hand was supposed to be lucky. I handed Rashid the money.

Rashid and I slipped into my mom's closet. The burka shimmered with rich gold fabric and thread. I tugged the stupid thing over my shirt and Levis. I could barely see with the mesh covering my eyes. The headband pinched my forehead and the hem dragged on the floor. I took three steps forward and fell over a footstool. "Ouch. No way," I muttered, flinging the stupid thing off. "Forget it, Rashid. I'll go dressed as I am."

"No. No do," Rashid said. "You want go for your friend, you wear."

"All right," I muttered. "But I'll put it on outside. It's too hot in here, I can't see in it, and I'm going to trip." I'd take Juma out, and tell my parents I was taking her for a walk and that I'd be a long time because I wanted to visit the O'Malley's down the street. When I got to the gate, I'd tie her up.

I stuffed the burka under my arm, leashed Juma, and left the house with Rashid. I secured Juma to the fence in the front yard. "Be good, girl. I'll be right back."

At the beginning of Nara Road, I forced the burka over my head. Rashid guided me along while the hem of the burka swept the street and sidewalks. I stubbed my toe on trash. Sweat rolled down my face when we got to the bus stop. Two men smoked, laughed, and talked beside us as we waited.

When the bus stopped, I pushed Rashid ahead so we could load but he shoved me back. Rude men pushed in front of me, not taking their turns. "Come on. Let's go," I whispered, shoving back.

"No wait," Rashid said. "And no English you say, 'Inshallah,' nothing else. And you go back of bus. You stand."

"What? No way. Aren't there any seats?" I attempted to throw the thing off so I could see the interior of the bus, but Rashid grabbed my hands.

"No, Runny. Wait."

"Let's take the next one if there's no room. But I want to stay by the door so I don't have to smell the exhaust."

"You go back," Rashid commanded. "And no English. Say 'Inshallah.' It means 'I angry,' okay?" What was Rashid trying to do?

"You liar. Inshallah means 'if God wishes'. I'm not stupid," I complained.

"No English, and you go the back, Runny. Or we no go," he said.

"Okay, okay, but Inshallah about the whole thing," I mumbled.

As I bumped up the metal grating of the bus stairs, a man pushed me aside. "Hey. Excuse you," I said as I grabbed Rashid to keep my balance.

"No. No English," Rashid whispered sternly.

When we entered the bus, I fumbled towards the back, which was packed with women—body against body. I slammed into one seat and a man pushed me aside. Someone else shoved me in the back and I stumbled forward banging my head into a seat. I winced but regarded Rashid's orders not to speak. Whirling around, I looked for him but another man blocked my way and roughly shoved me farther back. I passed some empty seats but moved on.

I remembered Rosa Parks, who had refused to sit in the back, but she'd also been arrested.

Before I got all the way down the row, the bus lurched forward, knocking me up against other women. The stench of curry, body odor, and bus exhaust was so strong I wanted to vomit. The headband of the burka itched and perspiration ran from my head. I tried to catch my breath as I slowly suffocated. Children ran across my feet as tired mothers tried to corral them. I bobbed and ducked my head trying to make out the figure of Rashid. I caught a glimpse of him toward the front before more women boarded the bus and boxed me in, crushing me in the crowd. I felt like throwing off the burka, pushing everyone aside and jumping off, but I had to get the note delivered for Frana.

The bus pitched back and forth throwing me against women. After what felt like hours, Rashid dragged me over feet and down the aisle. Someone pinched my butt and I wanted to turn back and punch the jerk. Rashid pulled me on. I fell down the steps and onto the curb. The hem of the expansive burka ripped; I knew Mom would kill me.

Walking became more difficult as the torn hem swept all the dirt and debris on the side of the street along with me. Finally, Rashid said, "This it. Stop here."

Darkness engulfed me and reaching out my hands, I felt the rough trunk of a tree next to a brick wall. "Where are we?" I felt a chill as I realized that I didn't know Rashid very well. He could easily leave me alone on the street.

"The Prime Minister house. The front up there," he said.

I threw off the burka. Rashid shoved me against the wall and completely into the shadow it cast. I squinted into the gloom and saw the wall loomed eight feet high with barbed wire on top. The tree's branches spread out over the wire.

"You wait here," Rashid said. "I climb tree."

"No. I have to go," I said. "I promised Frana."

Rashid shrugged and began to climb the tree; I climbed after him. When we got to the top, I threw the burka over the barbed wire, and used it to push the wire down. The burka stuck in the wire, we crawled along, and I cut my finger pulling it free. Mom would kill me unless I could slip it back into the closet undetected.

Rashid jumped nine feet down to the ground. I imagined the pain smacking my knee would cause. I closed my eyes, let go of the wall and dropped, banging my knees on the dirt as I landed.

We crawled across the yard. Rashid stopped behind some bushes. Would there be any guard dogs? My mind wandered to Juma at our gate.

I followed Rashid around the shrubs towards the side of the house. When we got to the side door, we noticed a mustached and armed guard in a gray uniform with red ribbons. We could turn back, but I remembered Frana's word, "You're the best friend I could have." We had to get to Shawnee.

Rashid approached the guard while I lay against the ground. *What a bad idea.* Rashid was the one who almost lost his hand because he stole a kabob. If he got arrested, how would I ever get home? I'd had to get the letter to Shawnee for Frana, but I wasn't prepared to die in a Pakistani prison.

I heard Rashid argue with the guard. *Oh, shoot. He was going to get himself in trouble.* They exchanged heated words and then I heard a laugh. I peeked out of the shadow and saw them walk around the corner and disappear. *Was the guard arresting Rashid?* After waiting for what felt like forever, I crawled to the door. Should I knock? I cautiously tried the handle. I leaned against the door. It swung open, throwing me to the floor. Rashid stood over me.

I scrambled to my feet. "How did you?" I stopped as I took in the splendor of the room. Polished wood floor peeked out from under thick Persian carpets and the walls were full of portraits of noble-looking men and women in golden frames. "Who let you in?"

"I give the guard some dollar. He like," Rashid said. "You come."

We mounted the wide stairs with the curving banister and turned down a long hallway at the top. At the first door, Rashid knocked.

Shawnee answered. His eyes widened. "Ronni, what are you . . .?"

I patted my hair and realized it was matted down with sweat. Great. So attractive. "I came with a letter from Frana." I handed him the letter. "The Shah's been overthrown. She has to flee to the U.S. She leaves tomorrow."

"She's going? Tomorrow?" His eyebrows furrowed and his eyes narrowed. He sighed so his shoulders slumped as he sat down to read. Tears formed in the corner of his eyes and he stopped, grabbed some paper, and started to write. My eyes burned. Shawnee really loved her, the way I wished someone loved me. "Will you take her a note from me?" I nodded, unable to speak. I felt guilty; their love made me feel so sad.

He gave me the letter, and I noticed that Rashid had disappeared again. A guard came to the door, and fear tightened my chest. The guard said something to Shawnee and Shawnee turned to me. "Some boy gave him money to have our driver take you home." *Rashid?*

I sat alone in the dark going home and wondered how I was going to sneak the tattered burka back into mom's closet. Then I wondered if Rashid would return. *Could I trust a thief with my money? I'd given him more than he could earn in a year. If he stole it, I didn't have any more money to buy Frana a gift.*

Juma was not in the front yard. In her place was a big hole. I snuck in the house and Dad sat in the living room. "Come in here," he called.

I attempted to hide the burka behind me. "What do you have behind your back?" he asked. I silently took the burka from behind my back. "Where have you been? Juma dug a hole in the front yard and barked so much she disturbed the entire neighborhood."

"I'm sorry," I answered. "I had to go for Frana."

"Your mother is furious and now you ruined her burka. You're going to have to pay for that with a year of allowances."

"I know. Why did Frana's dad come to you for help?" I asked changing the subject.

"Go to bed, Ronni," he said in a tired voice and I trudged up the stairs.

* * *

The next morning, a tap at my door woke me. Blurry-eyed, I glared at the clock—five a.m. I opened the door and Rashid handed me a little box. "Open," he said.

I pried off the lid. Inside lay a little silver Fatima's hand and a chain. "Where did you? How did you get this in the middle of the night? It's beautiful." I tried to hug him but he pulled away. Embarrassed, I realized he wouldn't want to be hugged by a girl. "Thank you," I said. He blushed and raced away.

By ten o'clock, I sat behind my mom in the car as the driver, Ahmed, followed a car with Frana's family inside. "Furthermore, you're never to borrow my clothes. My burka's ruined. You have no idea how much that cost. It's coming directly out of your allowance."

"Yeah. I know Mom. I'm sorry," I said. Served her right she didn't care about anyone but herself.

"You can't just take things. You don't respect anything. Every time I buy you new contact lenses you lose them. Why can't you be more like Amy?" She hated me. My own mother couldn't love me. I wished I could get on the plane with Frana.

I played with the box in my pocket and counted the minutes until we got to the airport. When we stopped, I bounced out of the car and found Frana. "I gave your note to Shawnee. He cried and he wrote this for you." I handed her the envelope he'd given me.

She tore it open. Tears misted in her eyes when she finished reading. "Thanks, Ronni," she said, hugging me. *Would she miss me as much as she'd miss him?*

Minutes before she had to board the plane, I pressed the box into her hand. "I got this for you."

She opened the box and twirled the little hand around in her palm. "It's great. I love it. Thank you. I got something for you too."

She gave me a small paper bag. There was a little silver basketball charm inside it. "For your bracelet," Frana said. "I want you to go out for basketball. I know we said we'd try out together but I won't be there, so you'll have to make some hoops for me."

I looked at my Sikh bracelet, our symbol of friendship, and held the basketball charm up to my charm bracelet. "I'm no good at team sports."

"You can do whatever you want to. Have fun. I'll be back when this all blows over. But be happy while I'm gone."

Before she boarded the plane, she turned and waved at me. No one would ever understand me like Frana did. Would I ever see her again? "The world is a small place, Ronni," she called. "There are always stamps and planes."

Sometimes, I thought as I walked away, it didn't feel small when the people you loved were on the other side of it. Would Frana be all right?

Chapter Thirteen

I had butterflies in my stomach the day of basketball tryouts. Frana's words, "You can do anything you want to," stayed in my mind. If I made the team, Mom would notice me. On one side of the gym, Amy gathered with her freshmen friends. She towered over them at five feet eleven inches tall in purple shorts. On the other side, I stood in my gym shorts feeling awkward, alone and short at five feet eight inches. I'd made a big mistake. I wished Frana were there.

Coach Campbell stood at the center court in the front in green shorts and an orange t-shirt. He had his black whistle cord wrapped around his hand.

We did drills: running back and forth, sprinting up and down. I beat Amy in running. But when we executed free throws, layouts, and jump shots, I didn't make as many shots as she did. After an hour, we scrimmaged. Coach Campbell pitted Amy and me against one another as centers on opposite teams. The whistle blew, the ball rose, we jumped, and Amy's hand struck the ball two inches above mine—of course. Her team won.

Afterward, Coach Campbell made a list of team members and positions. When I checked it, I saw Amy was center. My name didn't even make the list.

On the late bus home, members of the newly formed girls' basketball team sat in the front of the bus and sang, "Give a yell, give a cheer for the girls that drink the beer in the cellars of old I.S.I. and if Coach Campbell should appear, we'll say, Campbell, have a beer in the cellars of old I.S.I."

They sang all ninety-nine repetitions of the song. I wanted to scream, but more than that I wanted to crawl under my seat at the back of the bus. Frana was wrong—there were worse things than trying—there was failing.

Across the aisle from me sat another girl I'd never seen before tryouts. "Why are you back here?" I asked.

"Nothing to celebrate." She looked down at her hands. "I didn't make the team."

"Yeah, same here." I reached out a hand and put a smile on my face. "I'm Ronni. What's your name?"

"Ellen. Ellen Rhoades. I just moved here from Tehran. My mom is the new elementary school principal and my dad is a math teacher."

"Why'd you move in the middle of the year?" I asked even though only the year before I had moved in the middle of the year also.

"My parents got worried. There are a lot of anti-American demonstrations in Iran."

"My best friend, Frana, is from Iran. She had to leave. She's in the States. I'm a sophomore. And you?" I asked, moving over to her seat to join her.

"I'm a junior," she said.

*   *   *

After dinner that night, I went by Mom's room. I peeked through the partially-open door. Mom and Amy lay on the bed examining the basketball schedule. I knocked. I needed to have some sport to deflect the attention away from Amy. "Mom, I want to take tennis lessons. Remember when you said they were only fifty cents an hour here? I want to play."

She frowned and shook her head. "Tennis? Why tennis?"

I didn't want to tell her that I didn't have to make the team or that I needed a sport. I shrugged. "I've always wanted to play."

"The club is ten miles away. How are you going to get there? Gas is expensive." She sighed like I was really putting her out. "You've always been my expensive child—your teeth, your contact lenses, and now tennis. And don't think of bothering your father with this silly idea."

"I can ride my bike." I snapped. "And I'll pay for the lessons myself." I didn't need anyone's approval. I'd take care of myself. I didn't need her. With heads hung close, they continued to examine the schedule again as though I'd disappeared as I closed the door.

Walking down the hall, I almost ran over Rashid. "Ronni, what sad?" he asked.

"I'm not sad. I'm fine." I said, and ignored him as I went to my room and slammed the door.

That night, as I tried to calculate how much money I'd need to take lessons and to get a racquet, I heard a tap at my door. I flung it open, and my dad stood there holding two twenty dollar bills and an old wooden racquet. "Maybe you'll get a new racquet when you learn how to play. It will be our secret." Juma nosed in the door as he turned to leave.

I whispered, "Thank you." Juma climbed onto the bed with me and put her cold nose on my face. "I love you, girl," I whispered to her.

* * *

Ellen and I became good friends as I showed her around I.S.I. She convinced me to join the yearbook committee and I convinced her to take tennis lessons. But, she didn't like running after the ball so she begged off lessons after two weeks. I continued taking lessons by myself and dreamed that one day I'd compete at Wimbledon with people paying to see me play. Then my mom would say, "That's my daughter Ronni. We're so proud of her."

Chapter Fourteen

The two clay tennis courts lay at the foot of the hill on which the embassy stood. From one end of the courts, I could see the Himalayan Mountains covered with snow rising up into the sky. Beside the courts stood a little shaded dugout structure with benches.

At one o'clock every Saturday and Sunday, Abdul, the squat native tennis pro, watered the rust-colored clay, rolled it with a manual metal roller, and re-chalked the white lines. During this ritual, I hit a ball against the wall behind the dugout. Other than that, I spent most of the weekend days staining my white socks orange on the clay.

Abdul came to my shoulder, but his voice boomed loudly, especially when I frustrated him. "Watch the ball, Wonni!" he'd yell as the ball whizzed by my ear. "Turn your body!" as the ball hit me in the stomach. "Wun for it, Wonni!" as he hit it a mile away from me. "No, no, no, Wonni!"

"I was watching the ball. I just missed it. Can't you hit it closer to me?"

"No, Wonni. You took your eyes off of it. Wun, Wonni. Wun."

Between taking lessons I kept my eyes peeled for people who might need a person to hit with. Sometimes that took an entire day. Everyone seemed to have partners.

A few ladies played doubles in the afternoon, but I was more interested in John Schwab. He was in my class. His blond bangs fell into his brown eyes when he played. I'd never paid attention to him until he showed up on the court. He slammed the tennis ball and got every ball hit at him. When he played Abdul, I'd watch with a certain amount of satisfaction.

"Come on, Abdul, you could've hit that one," John joked after an overhead slam.

"What's wrong Abdul can't you run for that!" I yelled. Revenge was sweet.

One afternoon John asked me, "You want to hit?"

I looked behind me, expecting someone who could hit to be standing there, but no one was. "Me?" I asked. "No, no, I'm just a beginner."

He nodded. "I've seen you play. You can get it over."

Smiling but knowing my own limitation, I answered, "You're too good."

"Want to hit or not?"

He hit the ball to me every time for almost an hour before someone needed the court. As we walked off, he asked, "Are you going to that spring dance in two weeks?"

Was he asking me out? "I don't know. Maybe. I have to talk to Ellen. We may go."

"Do you want to go, well, maybe with me?"

I didn't have a date yet, but did I want to go with him? He was the kind of guy people didn't notice and I'd never be popular if I went out with him. "Maybe."

He flushed. "You know, just as friends and all."

Suddenly, I felt bad for him. Asking me out must have been hard, and I brushed him off. Poor guy. No way Matt would ask me. "Sure, I guess."

*   *   *

On April 4, 1979, a week before the spring dance, Ellen and I were riding our bikes to the tennis courts. Even though she no longer played, I was glad to have her there, cheering me when I competed. We reached a street with the grassy median that marked three miles left to go on our ride, and spotted a group of twelve women. Most of them wore the traditional shalwar kameez, loose pantsuits covering their bodies from wrists to ankles. Their heads were covered with scarves called dupattas and some had veils over their faces. Three women had totally covered themselves in tent-like burkas.

They huddled by the side of the road holding crude cardboard signs with pictures of Prime Minister Zulfikar Ali Bhutto, Shawnee's father. They wept in long, deep, wrenching sobs, one after the other.

I slowed down, "Look, Ellen. Is that Bhutto? What happened?"

"My mom said they executed Bhutto early this morning."

"Shawnee's father? He's dead?" I asked.

"Yes, they hanged him in Rawalpindi."

"Oh, my God. I wonder if Frana knows? Do you think Shawnee is okay? He was under house arrest. I have to write Frana."

* * *

At the spring dance, Ellen and I separated ourselves from our dates to talk beside the girls' locker room. Unfortunately, I wore the same turquoise dress that Amy had worn to the winter dance, but Mom had refused to have another made for me. She was still steamed over the burka incident. Amy, of course, had a new dress and had been asked by Luke. Ellen wore a pink sleeveless gown. We stood under the purple and gold balloons and streamers taped all over the gym and watched a dozen couples dance shoeless on the basketball court. I eyed the concession stand; Matt East stood by the cookies. He was home for the two-week spring break.

Pulling Ellen along, I walked towards Matt, allegedly for a cola. My dress looked good on me and I would casually bump into him. Before I reached him, Katie Leonard cut in front of us and ran into him. Katie, of course, wore a spaghetti-strapped red gown that matched her lipstick and nail polish. As I fumed, she flipped back her hair and parted her painted lips to give a full-throated laugh at something Matt said.

How did I expect Matt to see me when there was Katie? Matt would never see me with my metal mouth and face always breaking out. Why would he? Katie didn't have a problem in the world. Life stank.

I couldn't watch, so Ellen and I jogged into the locker room. We closed the door.

I whispered, "Did you see Katie flirting with Matt? Not that he minds. She doesn't even look our age."

"Come on, Ronni, you're prettier than she is." She reached over and patted my hair.

"Yeah, right. I'm afraid to smile without blinding people with the glare, my dress is used, and I can't even wear makeup yet." I felt like my whole life floated in the toilet bowl.

The door to the locker room opened letting in the blast of music and laughter. Ellen yelled to be heard.

"Oh, Matt, is my hair just right?" She batted her eyelashes and flipped her hair, "Oh, Matt...."

The door to the room had closed again so everyone heard her yell, "Oh Matt."

Two freshmen ran out of the bathroom giggling. *Oh, my God, I thought, what if Matt heard?*

Chapter Fifteen

The sign plastered to the wall next to the swimming pool read "lifeguard training." Under the word trainer, Matt East's name appeared. Finally, my chance to spend time with Matt and get a summer job had arrived. After I signed up, I handed the pen to Ellen.

"I can hardly swim. I can't save anyone. I'll leave the rescuing up to you," she said.

Practice began a week later. After treading water for five minutes, passing every rescue test, and holding my breath under water for three minutes, I became a junior lifeguard.

On my first day of lifeguard duty, Rashid brought me the bright yellow bikini the tailor had just finished. A look of disgust clouded his face while he held it out to me in my bedroom.

"Thanks. What's wrong with you?"

"Memsahib make me give," he explained. I remembered that our bearer, Muhammad, refused to wash our underwear and guessed that Rashid didn't like carrying the bikini because it resembled underwear. After he handed it off, he stood shuffling his feet before he said, "Memsahib, look me."

"Come in and hide," I said. "I'll change in the bathroom."

Just then the doorbell ran and in a moment Mom yelled up the stairs, "Ronni, Ellen's here."

I kicked a reluctant Rashid out so I could model my suit for Ellen. "Does it make me look too fat?" I asked, sucking in my stomach.

"No, you look great. Who told you you were fat anyway?"

"My family." My legs were muscular due to all the tennis I played but the insides of my thighs were too flabby.

She shook her head. "Well, they're crazy."

"Do you think . . ."

"Matt will think you look really sexy in that. Just watch out." She smiled. "He may get the wrong idea."

I slumped. "Yeah, sure. He won't even look at me."

"If he doesn't he's crazy. I don't see why you waste your time on that guy anyway. He isn't as great as you think he is. Besides he's too stupid to ask you out. I think the only reason you like him is because he's in college. You could get half a dozen guys in high school if you wanted." *Only chumps would look at me? Matt wouldn't.*

As I walked down the stairs, I saw that Mom had cornered Rashid. "Rashid, no more excuses. I need you to sit for me, today. I have to finish this pastel."

"No, Memsahib." He shook his head and backed away from her. "Much work."

"Work can wait."

"Mom, why don't you leave him alone? He doesn't want you to draw his picture. It's against his religion." I stepped in front of him, giving him a chance to slip out of the room.

"Rashid, where are you going?" Mom asked. "Ronni, you stay out of it. I've drawn a dozen Muslims and they never objected."

Ever since I could remember I hadn't had a say in whether I wanted to sit for her. When I was little I'd thought it was time she gave me to be with her, but maybe I'd just been a free model. I'd had enough. "That doesn't matter. Rashid doesn't want to sit for you; he shouldn't have to.

Your art is more important to you than anything else. You're so selfish."

"Ronnie, mind your own business. Since you can't treat me with respect, you can find your own ride to work."

"Thanks a lot. Now I'll be late on my first day." I stormed towards the door. I had to ride my bike if I wanted to get to the pool any where near the time I was scheduled.

As I toed up the kickstand, I remembered Ellen. I walked my bike over to her. "Sorry you had to see that. You didn't bring your bike by any chance did you?"

She shook her head. "Your mom was going to drive us."

"I'll ride you on the handle bars," I offered.

"Ten miles? No, you're in a hurry. I'll just call my mom."

"I'm sorry. I wish I could wait for you," I said. Ellen went back into the house while I pushed the bike towards the gate.

"Hi, Mr. Wasp," Ellen called behind me.

"Ronni, wait. I'll give you girls a ride," my dad called. "A job is a big responsibility. You should always be on time and work hard." We jumped in the Jeep and he lectured me on employment the rest of the way to the pool.

"I had planned on being on time. Mom was the irresponsible one," I defended myself.

I arrived for duty half an hour early and went for a swim while Ellen sat in the sun. Soon moms clutching romance novels filled the area among hordes of screaming kids. Matt arrived wearing his white cowboy hat; it covered the freckles sprinkled over his cheek and his nose. Next to Matt walked a tall, olive-skinned guy. The guy nudged Matt as they walked by and Matt stopped, looking down on me from the side of the pool. "Hey, Ronni, you work today?"

"You know I do," I said smugly. "You made the schedule." Was it my imagination or did his eyes linger on my bikini top a little longer than necessary?

"Yeah, well, I was just checking." Matt took a step but the guy nudged him again. "Oh, yeah. Ronni, this is Alex."

Alex bent over to shake my hand. "Hi, Ronni. I'm Alex." His hand was large and he was tall. His dark eyes seemed to stare through me.

"Yeah, Matt just said that," I answered.

"So you lifeguard with Matt, huh?"

"Yeah." I looked around for Matt, and saw him disappearing into the locker room. I wondered why he'd left me to entertain his friend.

"I'm here from Cornell University in New York," Alex said.

"Never heard of it."

"My dad's the Yugoslavian Ambassador."

"And how do you know Matt?" I said as I got out of the pool and maneuvered my way through the pack of children towards the locker room.

Alex followed. "We both went to I.S.I. our senior year, the year before last. You weren't here then?"

"No, I got here about a year ago."

"Are you a senior?"

"No, I'll be a junior this year," I admitted, thinking it was nice to be mistaken for older.

"How old are you?" Alex asked.

"What? Why do you want to know?" *Why was the guy cross-examining me?*

"Just curious?"

Another kid ran towards me and I dodged him, accidentally

bumping into Alex. "Don't run. You're going to fall and crack your head open," I said, as Alex put up his hands to keep me from colliding with him. I turned to Alex. "Sorry. Thanks." I walked out of his arms. "I'm sixteen. How old are you?"

"Nineteen." I turned away from him. "Hey, you want to go to a movie at the embassy theater some night?"

"Is Matt going?" I brightened. *This could be my way to get Matt to notice me.*

He frowned a moment. "Yeah, if you'd like."

"Fine," I said. If Matt were going, I'd be going out with Matt on a date—sort of.

I debated all week on whether to ask Alex if Ellen could go. Did college girls invite their friends? Would he think of me as a dumb kid? I lost my nerve and never asked.

Saturday night, Alex and Matt picked me up in Matt's blue bug. Alex opened my door. His black hair was slicked back against his scalp, looking wet and smelling of fabric softener; the odor blended with the strong smell of his Brut cologne and Wrigley Spearmint gum. At least he smelled good.

He wasn't shy; I found that out during the movie when his arm slowly slipped around my shoulders. I sat up so it dropped behind my back where Matt couldn't see it. If Matt saw Alex's arm around me, he'd think I liked Alex. He'd think I was unavailable. I glanced at Matt, but he stared straight ahead at the screen. He never noticed me. How could I get Matt to notice me? What did I have to do? The only time I'd ever been out with him and someone else asked me. I decided the heck with him. I leaned back and Alex reapplied his arm on my shoulder.

* * *

"It's only nine. You guys want to go to the club?" Matt asked, as we walked out of the theater after the movie.

I wiggled out of Alex's arm, which still encircled my shoulder. He stuffed his hands in his pocket.

"Yeah," I said. "Do you?"

"Yeah, I got some beer in my car," Matt said. A shiver of fear and excitement traveled down my spine. I didn't like the taste of beer, but if Matt wanted to drink, so would I. I'd do anything to make him like me.

We rode in Matt's bug down to the bottom of the hill. Matt unlocked the gate to the pool area and we slipped in. The only light came from the moon and the club dining room, across the lawn from the pool. The light hit the pool and gave it a deep glow. It felt eerie. Suddenly, a chill shot through me.

The orange-cushioned lounge chairs looked gray. Beyond, at the pool snack bar area, the moon shone through widely spaced wooden bars that shaded the tables during the day. Music escaped from the bar in the basement of the American Club. It didn't close until midnight. Occasional laughter filtered out to us, too.

I sat down on a damp cushion. Matt went into the snack bar and produced a candle and some matches. He placed a red cooler on the floor next to our chairs and got out a can of beer. "Alex, a brew?" he asked.

Alex looked at me. "You okay, Ronni? You look cold." He took off his jacket. "Here, have this."

"Ronni, want a brew?" Matt asked. Beer reminded me of my grandfather's breath. Yet if I didn't drink, what would Matt think?

Before I could answer, two shadows walked out of the darkness; one held the orange glow of a lit cigarette to her mouth—from their fingertips hung the shadows of beer bottles. As they walked by the pool, the other figure lit a cigarette. In the flare of the match, I saw Katie Leonard and another girl.

Darn, not Katie. She strolled over to us and put down her empty bottle. "You guys got some more?"

Matt opened one for each of the girls. "How did you guys get in the gate?"

"My sister, Jenny," Katie said, pointing to the other girl, "slipped through the bar and helped me hop the gate." She noticed me and said, "Hey, Ronni." She turned to Jenny and continued, "This is Matt. And I don't know him." She nodded at Alex.

Alex stood up and extended a hand in Jenny's direction. "I'm Alex. I attend Cornell. And you?" He waited for the girls to sit before he lowered himself back in his chair.

"George Mason. My second year. How about you, cowboy?"

"How'dy, George Mason too," Matt answered handing the girls beers.

My heart sank. First there was Katie and now her thin, blond, blue-eyed sister. How could I compete with a college girl from Matt's school?

"Anyone want a cig?" Jenny held the pack out.

Alex and Matt shrugged the idea off. "No," I said. "I don't want it on my breath when I get home." I sounded like a two-year old.

"Is that why you're not drinking?" Katie asked, picking up my beer.

"No. I just put it down." I took it from her and took a tentative sip.

Jenny took a swallow from her bottle and said, "If I drink enough of these, maybe we'll go skinny dipping."

Oh shoot. I wasn't going to do that—no way. I took a little sip of the beer.

Katie rolled a pack of Lifesavers over to me and winked. "For the breath."

About half an hour later, I started to laugh and tell jokes without punch lines. Everyone talked too fast and I couldn't stop giggling.

"Is she all right?" Jenny motioned toward me. I chuckled because she was so funny.

"How many did she drink?" Katie asked, raising her eyebrows at me.

Matt held up his finger. "Only one."

Katie took my beer from me. "It's almost empty."

I smiled at her. "I'll have another, please." I almost fell out of my seat laughing.

"No," Alex said, taking my hand and pulling me to my feet. "We've got to take you home. It's already ten-thirty."

"No! Can't we go to the club and dance? Come on, Matt, let's go dance." I walked toward Matt thinking I would kiss him. He'd hold me real tight, kiss me back, and tell me he'd always loved me.

Alex grabbed me by the shoulder and kissed my cheek. "No, babe, you're too young to get into the club." I flinched away from him. He turned and held a hand out to Matt. "Matt, give me your keys. I'll take her home."

I pushed Alex away. "No, if Matt stays, so do I." I knew everything I was saying was stupid, but I couldn't stop myself. "You want to dance, right?" I asked Matt.

He rose from his chair. "No, I have to go, too. I have to work tomorrow."

I chewed Lifesavers and laughed the whole way home. I staggered out of the car and Alex had to help me to the door. Alex leaned in to kiss me. I stepped back and put up my hands. "Good night." I opened the door and closed it on him.

"Good night. I had a good time," he called through the closed door. A light shone in the living room and I sobered up quickly.

"Ronni, come in here," my dad called. He had waited up for me.

I leaned around the entrance to the living room holding onto the doorjamb for balance. "Oh, you're up," I said cheerily. "Good night."

He tapped his watch. "It's pretty late to be getting home."

Shoot. Did he know I'd been drinking? I stayed out of the room, away from him. "Yeah, I, I went to a movie, you know, at the embassy, the movies, you know."

"Next time you go out, I want to meet your friends. And you need to come home at a decent hour." He pushed his reading glasses up on his nose.

"I'm not a baby. It's not a school night." I glared at him. "Everyone else gets to do whatever they want. They get treated with respect."

"Go to bed, Ronni." He didn't even look up from his magazine.

I stormed up the stairs. He wasn't going to ruin my chance with Matt.

Chapter Sixteen

The next day, Alex called and asked me out on a double date for the next weekend; Matt and Katie Leonard would be with us. I almost declined but something made me say yes. *Did I just want to be near Matt? Why? Matt liked Katie. Why would he like me? Compared to her I was a dog. Why couldn't my life be more like hers?*

Alex said we would go to the American Club to eat. As I got ready, I heard Mom's footsteps descending the stairs and decided to borrow some of her makeup. As I pushed open the door, I heard someone behind me and stared. Rashid stood there. "Oh, Rashid." I pressed my hand to my chest as if to stop it jumping out. "Hey, you can help me out." I positioned him by the door. "Call to me if anyone comes."

I snuck into the room and rummaged through Mom's lipsticks, hairbrushes, eye shadows. Maybe if I wore some, Matt would see me. My hand shook as I combed mascara through my eyelashes. She wouldn't be able to tell. I picked up some bright red lipstick and swiped it over my lips. *Wow. Too bright.*

Rashid called, "Memsahib, I come." Darn. I grabbed a tissue and fled the room rubbing my lips.

As I headed back to my room, the doorbell rang. I listened as my dad opened it. "Hello, sir," I heard Alex say. I peered down the stairs and saw Alex put out his hand for my father to shake.

"Now you bring her back early. Last time she was out too late. Nine o'clock is the curfew. Do you understand?"

Alex nodded his bent head and shuffled his feet. "Yes, sir. Sorry about last time, sir."

I was mortified, my face burned as Alex held the door open for me and I got in the backseat. My stomach turned; Matt's breath reeked of beer. *Well, I would pass on that; I'd made a big enough fool of myself the last time we went out.*

When we pulled up in front of the Leonard house, Matt said, "Alex, you go meet the folks. I don't want them to know I've been drinking. You know how parents get about that."

"Maybe Alex should drive," I suggested. Matt flashed his eyes at me and I regretted speaking.

Katie's father came out of the house with her. A tall, tanned man, Mr. Leonard combed his hand through his sandy hair and I noted how striking his resemblance was to his daughter. I'd seen him at the tennis courts a couple times. He was one of the top men's players. He waved at us and called, "You kids have a great time."

When Katie got in the front seat next to Matt and her dad had gone inside, Matt handed her a beer, and we took off. "Ronni," Matt said. "Did you hear that we're showing *Star Wars* at the pool next week?"

I swallowed my fear that Matt was too drunk to drive. "Yeah, my dad told me. It's in honor of the Chinese Ambassador." Oh no, I sounded like a real geek—my daddy said.

"If you want to work it, I can schedule you in?" he said.

"That's fine." Maybe the makeup worked; Matt spoke to me.

"It's about time we got a new movie." Katie took a gulp of her beer. "We never see anything that hasn't already been out two years in the States."

"Yeah, just imagine what would happen if we befriended Russia.

Maybe they'd send over a McDonalds," I said. Alex laughed.

"I wish," Matt said. "I'm sick of that old tough, starved-to-death water buffalo they pass off as hamburger in the snack—".

Crunch. Bang. Screech. The car spun like the Mad Hatter's Teacup, out of control. Tree. Sky. Tree. Sky. I heard myself scream. Glass flew and we smacked against something, jolted, and stopped.

An eerie pause filled the car. I heard nothing; as though my ears didn't work. I took inventory of myself and my mouth had bits of glass in it. The realization crept over me that we had been hit. I was alive but what about Matt, Katie, and Alex?

Matt groaned. "What the hell was that?" Katie leaned forward and I saw her between the front seats.

"Everyone okay? Let's get out." Matt opened his door and metal grated on metal.

"Come on, Alex," I looked toward the curb on his side. He didn't move. Blood flowed down his paper-pale face and his head collapsed into the metal of the doorframe. He wasn't moving. Oh, my God, he was dead? I pushed up Matt's seat and leapt out of the car and onto the street.

Suddenly, a sharp pain stabbed me in the shoulder and traveled down my arm. "Alex isn't moving!" I yelled.

Matt leaned into the back seat. "He's breathing! He's alive."

Thank God. I tasted the metallic flavor of my own blood. I swiped at my nose and felt sticky blood on my fingers. It gushed from the side of my nose.

I checked out Katie and Matt. Her lip swelled to the size of a golf ball and bled, and he had angry scratches over his eye and left cheekbone.

A car screeched to a halt. I staggered to the curb and sat down. I felt sick to my stomach and began to shiver. Someone said, "We're calling the Yugoslavian Embassy. We need to air-lift this boy out of here, now."

"Is he going to be all right?" I whispered. No one answered.

Two emergency workers from the British Embassy got Alex out of the car and placed him on a blanket on the ground. They covered his face with a towel, which soon turned crimson as blood saturated it. "Oh, God, don't let him die," I pleaded. Alex had been kind and I had repaid this with rudeness.

"Are you all right?" a man with a Canadian accent asked.

"My shoulder hurts and I think I swallowed some glass."

"You have a cut on the side of your nose. Must have the doctor look at that. I'll ask your mum and dad if I can take you to the doctor."

"They're not here."

"Well, shouldn't I be calling your mum then?"

Great. Mom would kill me when she found out Matt was drunk. I gave the man my phone number and he took off.

Down the street, smashed and turned around backwards, I saw a black four-door car with all the glass broken out of the windows and windshield. That car must have hit us, I thought. A crowd gathered around it as well. Someone asked Matt if we were with the American Embassy.

The Canadian man who'd questioned me came back. "We'll be taking you to the doctor. Your dad will meet you there."

He drove me to the medical office within the embassy compound. The last time I'd been in the medical office, I'd received my rabies booster. Since my encounter with that shot, I feared needles. Dad arrived and sat silently next to me while I stared at a long needle that would stitch up my nose. The doctor told me I needed a sling and two cosmetic stitches on the right side of my nose. He couldn't do anything about the glass I swallowed.

As I left the clinic, Katie and her father walked in; with them came a smell of martinis and suntan oil Katie called to me, "Ronni, you okay?"

"I'm fine. Did they take Alex? Is he okay?"

"They air-lifted him out. He's unconscious," Katie's father said.

Katie's father and mine stood talking about golf while Katie went in to see the nurse. I needed to get away to think. "I'm going down to the tennis court a moment," I told my dad.

"Okay, I'll only be a minute."

The dugout was deserted; I sat in it and cried. *How could I be so stupid? I let Matt almost kill me. And Alex. What if Alex died? Drinking and driving. What would mom say?*

A minute later, a tap on my shoulder surprised me. My dad stood over me with a wrinkled brow. "Are you in pain?" he asked, putting a hand on my uninjured shoulder.

I swiped at tears. "No, I'm ready to go."

"What happened? Are you sure you're okay?"

"Matt, he was drinking and Alex . . . What if he dies? I shouldn't have—"

"It's not your fault, Ronni." He squeezed my good shoulder. Maybe he really loved me. I hurt everyone who cared about me. Look at what I did to Alex. He might die because I wanted to date Matt. Would my dad still love me if he knew Alex was on a date with Matt because of me? Alex could die because of me.

"I know how it feels to think you're responsible for hurting other people," Dad said. I smiled up at him. "It was 1961, a year before I married your mother. I worked in the Dominican Republic and I'd go out and meet the local farmers but my contacts kept disappearing. The government finally sent me home because Trujillo, the country's dictator, thought I was FBI investigating the murder of Galíndez."

How could anyone mistake my mild-mannered dad for a spy? I squinted up at him skeptically.

"It's true. Galíndez was a New Yorker who wrote about Trujillo's tyranny and in 1960 he was kidnapped, tortured, and killed."

"How is that your fault?" I asked.

"When I talked to farmers, they disappeared. Because I talked to them, Trujillo had them imprisoned or killed."

"You didn't know."

"And you didn't know Alex would get hurt."

Chapter Seventeen

When we got home, Mom and Amy met us in the entranceway. "What happened? Are you okay?" Mom asked. "Did you eat? Dinner's ready."

"I'm fine, but I'm not hungry." I marched up to my room.

About half an hour later, there was a soft knock at my door. Rashid tiptoed in and handed me five chocolate chip cookies. "You no eat. You like cookies."

"Thanks, but I'm not hungry."

"Why? You hurt your skin and hand." He pointed to the stitch in my nose and my shoulder.

I remembered how he almost lost his hand the day I met him. "Yeah."

There was a knock and Rashid dove under the bed as I called, "Come in."

My dad stood in the doorway. "Your friend is on the phone."

"What friend?"

"I don't know. A girl." *Leave it to my dad to not remember the name of any of my friends.*

I ran to get it. "Hello?"

"Ronni. Ellen. I heard about the accident. Are you okay?"

"I jammed my shoulder. I think Alex's head hit it before the doorframe hit him. It was awful. I swallowed glass and got stitches for a cut in my nose. Alex is unconscious."

"You want to come over and spend the night tonight? My mom got some water buffalo milk. You can help us take turns cranking the ice cream maker."

We didn't get regular milk, but buffalo milk tasted pretty close though I don't think it was pasteurized and it took hours to prepare ice cream, cranking the machine until it got solid. "I can't crank anything with my arm, and I don't really feel like it tonight, but thanks. I'm just tired."

"Come on, Ronni. We can escape to my room and talk if you want."

My dad drove me over to Ellen's house. "Did you know I played baseball?" Dad asked. When I didn't answer, he continued, "I did. My parents were poor and I couldn't get new shoes. I grew out of mine and they pinched my toes, but I played any chance I got." I pushed back the urge to cry. "When I got a scholarship to the University of Maine, I went to try out for their team. I found the coach's door and there was a sign with the names of the players. My name wasn't on it. I didn't get a chance to try out." At least I got to try out for basketball.

"I'm sorry," I said biting my lower lip.

"It was okay," he said. "There was an intramural team and I played on that." He touched my arm. "You'll be able to play tennis again soon."

When we pulled up to the curb in front of the American Compund, my da added, "I still love to go watch the University of Maine team play whenever we get back home."

I waved briefly when I got out and watched him drive away. *I hadn't known he loved baseball. He knew how important tennis was to me, but I was too self-centered to know him. I'd done so much wrong; hurt too many people. Could I ever make it right?*

Ellen's one-story apartment was much smaller than ours. When I got inside, Ellen and I went straight to her room.

"Okay. What happened to Matt and Katie?" She flopped on the bed.

I began to cry. "Matt was drinking and Alex might die just because I wanted to go out with Matt."

She put her arm around my shoulders. "Matt knew what he was doing. You didn't force him to drink and drive."

"But you don't understand. Alex only went on the double date because I wanted Matt along."

"I don't know why you like that guy. He's trouble."

"Something's wrong with me. When I came here, I had a boyfriend in Morocco and he wrote a few times, but now he's forgotten me. Then Frana had to leave. Any guys who are nice to me, I'm mean to."

"You still have friends. Let's make a pact. Friends first. Whatever happens we think of our friends first. We should only date guys who have friends so we can double."

"Don't remind me of double dating. But I'll stick to high school guys. Are there any good ones out there?"

"Ian likes you. You should date him. Or how about John—you both play tennis."

"Ian likes everyone and John's boring."

Ellen's mom came in the room with two bowls of ice cream, honey, and cookies. Ellen and I made our pact over dessert and we went into the living room where we laughed and talked. Then we turned on the television and sang along with a commercial jingle, "Mitchell's peas are good for you. Mitchell's peas are good to eat." A Pakistani woman took a big spoonful of peas and the commentator said something in Urdu; we laughed some more. We fell asleep around midnight.

*   *   *

Matt didn't show up at the pool the next day. Ellen and I grabbed a couple of colas from the snack bar. "I heard Matt's been sent back home," she whispered. "That way he doesn't have to go on trial and the embassy saves face."

"Did they even test his alcohol level or Katie's?"

"I don't know."

"What about poor Alex? He could die because of Matt."

"I heard he's in Yugoslavia, and he's still in a coma," Ellen said.

A hand clamped onto my good shoulder and I jumped. "How's your arm?" Ian asked.

"Good, I guess, but I can't work or anything. I can't get the sling wet."

"Maybe you can get a job in a freak show. The black string looks weird coming out of the side of your nose," Ellen laughed.

"I think it looks sexy." Ian pinched my arm. "What's the scoop anyway?"

"Ronni doesn't want to talk about it." Ellen took a gulp of her cola.

"Okay. So maybe I'll show you guys my latest card trick." Ian scooped up a pile of cards someone had left on a nearby table. Soon we played gin rummy. I could always count on Ian to make me feel better about any situation.

Rocky, the Marine who'd eavesdropped on my conversation with Juma, and one of his fellow Marines, a new guy, stopped at our table. "Hey, Ronni-I-gotta-go, how are you?"

Shoot, Rocky was never going to let me live down my past. "Hi," I said, hoping he'd leave.

The new Marine grinned at Ellen. "Hi. What are you guys playing?"

"Gin," I said.

"My names Kevin." He extended his hand first to me and then to Ellen. "What happened to your arm?" he asked, still looking at Ellen.

Ellen told him the whole story, and Kevin and Rocky sat down to play cards with us. Kevin sat by Ellen and spent more time talking to her than concentrating on his hand. She kept flipping back her hair and staring at him.

It didn't take her long to forget our pact. "Are you guys going to the movie next week?" I asked.

"Who isn't?" Ian said. "Even the Chinese Ambassador."

I glared at Ellen as she placed a hand on Kevin's arm. "What is our problem with China anyway?" I bet the Chinese were more loyal than Ellen who seemed to completely forget that we had promised to put friends first and not to go for older guys.

"Well, we sold arms to Taiwan and that made China angry," Kevin said. "But, President Carter did sign a treaty with China in January against Congress' vote to not establish relations with China at Taiwan's expense. But we've established diplomatic ties so here we are."

"You know it gets pretty hard to know who we have to hate," I said. "If they eat pork and worship Brahma, the Muslims don't like 'em and if they eat cow and worship Allah, the Hindus hate 'em. If they're socialists, we hate 'em, and they hate us for being capitalist. If they share the same homeland but not religion they hate each other, too. At school we should have to wear name tags so we know who to hate." I glared at Ellen.

Before the Marines left, Kevin asked Ellen, "How about we go out on a double date? We could double with Ronni and Ian."

"He's not my boyfriend," I said.

"God, that hurts," Ian teased, hugging me on my good side.

The next day, after meeting Ellen at the pool and watching her go off with Kevin to get something to eat, I escaped to the tennis courts again. Ellen had said friends first, but what about deserting me to go off with this new older guy?

I borrowed Abdul's racquet and a ball even though I knew I couldn't play—not with my right arm in a sling. I tried to hit the ball against the wall with my left hand. I wanted to slam it, but I swung and missed again and again. It was no use. All those days and hours on lessons wasted. I couldn't play. Maybe never again.

I heard footsteps behind me. "Your friend, Ian, told me I might find you down here," my dad said. "What are you doing with the racquet?" He had Juma with him; she jumped up to greet me.

"Hi, girl. I thought I might be able to play with my left hand," I said. "But I can't."

"I bet you can learn. Look how well you learned with you right. All it takes is practice."

"No. I'm already tired."

"Come on." He motioned for the dog to sit on the sidelines and tossed me the ball. I missed it over a dozen times. Then I started to make contact. He kept tossing until the sun slipped behind the horizon.

"I did it," I said. I felt like dancing and singing. I hugged my dad.

He pulled away and looked down at the dog. "Yes. Now let's go home." He whistled and Juma ran to us. She jumped up on my bad arm and Dad pulled her off. When we got in the Jeep, Juma draped herself over my lap and we drove home.

*   *   *

When I got home from school the next day, I realized I wasn't the only one whose love life was all in her head. I found an envelope and a letter next to the lamp in the living room. The envelope was addressed to Donny Osmond. It was from Amy Wasp. I unfolded the letter, as Amy entered the room with a stamp.

It read: *Dear Donny Osmond.*

Amy rushed toward me. "Hey, give me it. It's mine."

I took off for the stairs. She followed, but I blocked her with my back and read it out loud. "Dear Donny. I love the color purple too." I hooted with laughter.

"Give it back! I'll tell." She shoved me into the banister.

"My dad says I'm a good Mormon girl. Oh, my God—you liar." I nudged her back with my hip.

She pushed me, so I held the letter out over the rail and used my free hand to push her back and went on reading. "I have a mole on my left cheek too. Amy, tsk, tsk, you shouldn't be dishonest."

"Shut up, it's mine! I'm going to steal your diary."

Rashid darted in and stood below me in the entryway. I waved the letter. "Here, Rashid, take the letter and don't give it to Memsahib Amy. She's a bad Shiite. It says so it the letter."

He held out his hand, but just then the front door opened, and Dad marched in, clutching his briefcase. Rashid scurried away towards the kitchen.

"Yoo-hoo, Daddy dearest," I hooted. "Your Mormon daughter wants to tell you something."

"Give it back," Amy shrieked. "Dad, she stole my letter."

Dad didn't even look up. "Not now," he muttered. He climbed the stairs, his head down, his white knuckles taut around his case. He didn't even glance at us as he edged past.

"What's wrong?" I asked.

He ignored me and walked up the rest of the stairs.

"Dad," Amy whined. "Ronni stole my letter. She's always stealing my stuff."

"Later. I'm busy," he growled.

He slammed his office door. *Something was wrong? Why was he so upset?*

Amy punched my arm. "I'll get you for this."

I dropped the stupid letter and started up the stairs. She seized it and followed on my heels. When she got to her bedroom, she slammed her door.

At the door to my dad's study, I stopped and knocked. He didn't answer. "Can I come in?" I asked through the panel.

"What?" he asked.

I opened the door. "Is something the matter?"

He sat in his large brown easy chair with a yellow legal pad in his lap. "Nothing that concerns you," he snapped. "I need to do some paperwork. You and your sister need to be quiet."

Mom was with the Pakistani Art Council, sketching in Moenjodaro. *Had something happened to her?* "Is it Mom?" I asked.

"No." He sighed. "Today the embassy in Iran was overrun by students. They took hostages."

"What? What does that mean?" I asked. "Could it happen here?"

"No. Our government supported the Shah and now he is seeking medical treatment for cancer in the States. The Ayatolla is angry, as are other Iranian citizens. Pakistan and the U.S. have a friendlier relationship. It's nothing. It'll be over soon. I have paperwork. Close the door when you leave."

No one knew that the Soviet Union would attack Kabul when we were there for the Cultural Exchange either. People shot at us. *How could we know for sure we were safe?*

Chapter Eighteen

The next day, I walked around the block to a little tin hut that sold candy and trinkets. I craved a large chunk of chocolate, but bought some gum instead. A month earlier when I had purchased a candy bar it had been full of squirming white maggots; the memory still made my stomach turn.

I shoved several sticks of the hard stale gum in my mouth and nearly broke a tooth chopping down on it. At least it was sweet.

As I left the shop, I almost bumped into Rashid. He clutched a bag as big around as he was. "Hi," I greeted him. "Where are you going?"

"I walk home," he explained.

"Walk. How far is it?"

"I live Rawalpindi. Ten and nine kilometers." He tugged on the bag and looked like he would topple over.

I did the math in my head and figured that nineteen kilometers was about twelve miles. "That's far." How would he make it with his bag? "Why don't you take the bus?"

"Bus go short way. I save rupees," he explained.

Just then Katie rode up in a canyon-red Chrysler Le Baron convertible. Her sister was at the wheel. Katie hung out the window and waved. The car stopped. "You need a ride?"

My house sat around the corner but maybe I could get them to take Rashid. "Where are you going?"

"We're just taking a ride. Come on." She waved me in. "Get in."

"Okay, maybe you could drive Rashid home." I pointed him. "He lives near Rawalpindi, about ten miles from here."

"Who's he?" she said, frowning at him as though he were a spider.

"He works for us." I had to think of a way to get her to agree. "I wanted to talk to you about the accident, but I have to find him a ride first."

The sisters looked at each other and Katie leaned over to whisper something in Jenny's ear. Then Katie looked back at me. "Okay. Hop in." We got in the back.

Jenny gunned the car and Katie leaned over the seat. "So, did you hear about Matt? He can't come back to Pakistan, but he won't be prosecuted."

"I heard that Alex is still unconscious," I said. I didn't want to think about my stupid crush on good-for-nothing Matt. "How's your lip?"

We roared out of town and buildings started to fade away, replaced with fields and mud huts. Rashid told us to turn down a dirt road. The wheels sank into potholes and clods of dirt flew up at us, Katie cursed and muttered, "Where is the place anyway, Mars?"

The farmhouse was three adobe brick structures with mud slopped over them, modern wooden doors, and wood and glass windows. A stick and straw animal pen ran alongside the main house. Long-eared goats with eyes spread far apart and bony foreheads called, "baahaa," as they pulled at ropes secured to a blossoming jacaranda tree. Rashid pushed on Katie's seat as if trying to jump from the car as we parked. "This my home, Runny. This my home."

An upright wheel-like contraption stood in the center of the yard. Two robust oxen, tethered to a rope, lumbered around in a circle making the wheel move. A thin old man fed green stalks into the wheel contraption. A metal trough was connected to other side of the wheel. The trough led into a cave-like hut a few feet away. What were they making?

Rashid pointed. "Look, Runny. I work. I buy new goat."

"Wow, a goat," Jenny said sarcastically. I smiled and hoped Rashid didn't hear her.

A middle-aged man strode towards us with his eyes squinted until he spotted Rashid, then he waved so that the long arm of his shalwar kamees, long, loose pajama-like clothes, flapped like a flag. "Salaam," he said flashing us a grin full of metal from replaced rotten teeth. "Come, come," he continued.

He walked by two women squatting at the side of the house. The older woman balled dough in her hand and slapped it onto the side of a hole in the ground. The dough flattened out into a chapati, or thick tortilla-like bread. I'd seen bread made before when my mom forced us to go on a sketching expedition with her.

As we passed, I peered in the hole. There was a fire in the bottom. I wondered why the bread didn't fall into the flames. The other woman gingerly flipped over a second chapati. "Salaam," I greeted the women. Neither spoke to me. The older one hid behind her dupatta so that only the silver strands of hair over her tan and wrinkled forehead showed above the veil.

"What a crap hole. Welcome to the *Beverly Hillbillies*," Jenny said. I wanted to punch her in the mouth for being so rude. Instead, I looked at Rashid. He smiled ear-to-ear, seemingly unaware of how derogatory she was being toward his home.

"That my father," Rashid said. "Come in, you see."

"We can't stay," Katie said, backing away.

"Please, I want show Runny." We passed through the door and entered the dwelling, which was surprisingly normal inside with a couch, table, and chairs.

"My father wife, she make pacora. You eat. You eat," Rashid said.

His father pushed aside the woven cloth that separated the rooms and disappeared a minute. The sound of pot and pans falling came from a back room, and Rashid's father returned, towing a reluctant young woman after him. The wife appeared to be about my age. She pulled away laughing, covering her mouth with her dupatta. He bowed his head towards us and said, "My wife—she purdah." My dad told me some woman practiced purdah and wouldn't go out without wearing a burka.

"That's your mom, Rashid?" I asked. She couldn't be old enough.

"No, father three wife. My mother chapatis." he explained, pointing toward the door.

"What a culture," Katie snorted.

"Ian would love being a Muslim. He could have as many women as he wanted," I joked.

"No, Ian just needs the right woman," Katie answered smiling. *What? Did she think she was the right one for Ian?*

Rashid showed us a table my mom had thrown out. I assumed he had salvaged it from the garbage to bring home. On the wall hung some sketches mom had done and discarded. He had saved them from the garbage too—a graveyard to the scarified souls. Things my family threw away, he treasured.

"We're not staying here long," Katie said.

I nodded and looked around. Mom would love to see this. She'd have insisted on sketching Rashid's three mothers. I imagined the rough off-white walls of the farmer's home decorated with a picture of the wife who hid in the kitchen to avoid being seen. The picture would never change. I remembered Oscar Wilde's book *The Portrait of Dorian Gray*—the portrait aged but the man never did. He cheated time and mortality. *What if what Rashid believed was true? What if, with each picture you lost a bit of your soul, the price for your memories?*

My thoughts were interrupted when a tall, solemn-looking guy walked in. Rashid smiled broadly and pointed to the young man. "Runny, this my brother, Muhammed. He go the University."

"Hi," I said.

Muhammed ignored me and shouted at Rashid. Rashid's father shuffled off to the back room. Muhammed shoved Rashid backwards and stormed off.

"I sorry. My brother. He don't like your Jimmy Carter." *What was wrong with Jimmy Carter? First, Kevin said the Chinese were mad at the President and now the Pakistani people, too.*

"He doesn't like us because of our president, Jimmy Carter? That's crazy," I said to Rashid.

Rashid insisted we sample several golden brown chapati, then took us outside to see all the animals and the weird wheel contraption. As we approached the wheel, I smelled molasses. I peered into the trough and saw brown sugar juice flowing towards the little hut. We went into the hut and watched the sugarcane juice gather in a large pan over a fire. Rashid's mother fed the fire with discarded sugarcane stalks.

Rashid grabbed a stalk and swirled it in the thick brown syrup. He pulled it out and handed it to me. It looked like a large brown lollypop. "Here, Runny. You like," he said. I licked the warm sweet treat while Rashid made two more for the other girls.

"That is so cool, Rashid. Your family has its own little candy shop and you even recycle the sugar cane stalks to heat up the sugar," I said.

He grinned and began to make a lollipop for himself. The moment ended when Muhammed burst in the hut. "Get out of here. You go. Leave." He snatched the lollipops from Katie and Jenny. I moved away from him as he came towards me.

Why did that guy hate us so much? "What did I do to you?" I backpedaled out the door of the hut as he stormed toward me.

He stood in front of me, glaring with hatred in his eyes. "You're not welcome. Go now."

I stood paralyzed as Jenny and Katie slipped out of the hut behind me. Jenny yelled, "You stupid S.O.B.," at Muhammed.

Rashid attempted to slip between his brother and me. "Runny. Sorry. You go. Thanks the ride." I walked backwards, keeping an eye on Rashid and Muhammed. Muhammed looked like he was going to rush us, but instead he pushed Rashid aside and threw stones at our feet as I turned and dashed for the car. Jenny roared away, flipping him off through the dust thrown up behind the tires. Rashid ran after us, waving. I sucked on the sweet sugar lollipop trying to forget about the fear welling up in my chest.

*   *   *

A week later, death, like a toe dipped in the water, started small— "Mr. Leonard killed himself," Mom whispered to Dad. *Katie's father? He killed himself. But why?* Death began to ripple out and spread. "His family found him this morning. Can you believe it?" Mom shook her head. I looked at Dad, but death was not for children so he ignored me.

Later, when I got to the pool, the story swelled from a tiny wave to a tsunami; everyone talked at once. "Katie found him in the bathtub. Blood was everywhere. He was CIA," Luke said.

"No one is supposed to know who was CIA. But I heard he was involved with the Shah and Savak," Ellen said. "They had people killed."

"Maybe, you know." Ian put his arm around my shoulder. "Was Mr. Leonard CIA?" He looked at me. I glared at him, confused, and he continued, "Since your dad is—."

"My dad's what?" I asked. *Was he going to say my dad was CIA? No way. I pushed away the doubts: We did leave Morocco quickly, he did help Frana's father and what about that information about Iran and Dr. Khan, the nuclear engineer in Pakistan?* I shook my head. My dad was a nerd, not a spy. He couldn't be; wouldn't I know?

"Nothing," Ian said patting my back and averting his eyes. "The CIA doesn't kill people. We're Americans, not some crazy foreign savages."

"What do we do now? A movie by the pool? Stay up all night?" Ellen asked.

We didn't mention that the girl who never seemed to have a care, never had a zit, never needed braces, and who flirted so easily with all the guys, was going home to bury her dad. What secrets cut so deep that you would die for them? People who were CIA weren't supposed to tell or else they'd have to leave the country. *What did Ian know? How could I find out? What if I didn't even really know my own father? Did my dad have secrets he kept from me?*

Chapter Nineteen

The next day Ellen dragged me with her to visit Kevin at his barracks. All she wanted to do was hang around with him. We sat on a green vinyl couch that our sweaty skin stuck to. Natural light filtered into the room through the three large tic-tac-toe-shaped windows. The shadow on the floor resembled prison bars. The muted mumble of a local news channel hummed from the television which balanced on a lame end table that, like all the other furniture in the room, looked roughly sandpapered by time. Other than that, the dull white room looked sterile. There were no books and magazines piled up on the end table and no carpet on the beige vinyl floor.

Ellen sat with Kevin's arm draped around her shoulder, and his white stockinged feet and legs wrapped around hers. They'd been inseparable. I was a third wheel. I wondered if Ellen even cared whether I tagged along.

Just as I thought I might as well leave, Ellen finally acknowledged my existence and asked, "Doesn't Kevin have the cutest accent? He's from New York—that's why they call him New York."

I forced a little grin. They'd become a couple awfully fast.

Rocky sat to my right on one of two wooden chairs. Each leg had a black rubber stopper to shield the chipped ends from the floor. The uneven legs rocked beneath him every time he shifted his weight.

He pointed to the small black and white television screen. "Look, those bastards are pulling out a hostage." A group of turban-wearing gun-slinging Iranians shoved four blindfolded hostages out into what looked like a street full of spectators. The language spoken wasn't English.

Rocky shuffled his feet, rubbing gray socks over the mirror-like vinyl floor. A groove had been worn down the middle of the floor where black dress shoes had traveled many times a day on their way to guard duty. "God, I'd like to have a rifle," Rocky muttered. "I'd pop them between the eyes. Why can't our government go in there and get them out?"

Kevin untangled himself from Ellen and bent forward. "They need to get us in there to kick some butt."

Ellen leaned over, grabbing his arm. "Wouldn't you rather stay here with me?" He leaned back and kissed her.

"Why don't we just send our soldiers in and take the embassy back?" I asked.

Rocky knotted his brow. "Yeah, right," he spat. "They'd kill the hostages." He shook his head and muttered. "Kids!"

"Shut up. I'm sixteen, Ellen is seventeen, and Kevin, or New York, whatever you call him is nineteen. You're just old."

"I'm twenty-one," he informed me dryly.

"Okay, you two," Kevin interrupted.

Ellen snuggled up against Kevin's gray t-shirt. "What do they want anyway?'

"The Shah's in New York, home sweet home, getting treated for cancer."

"So, let's send him back," I said. "It's their dispute, let them handle it."

Rocky stood up and paced in front of me. "Yeah, right. Here, terrorist, we'll give you what you want. Please don't hurt us."

I freed myself from the sweaty clutches of the couch and jumped up. "He's sick. Maybe they'd have pity on him. That's better than letting sixty innocent people suffer."

"Terrorists don't know what pity is."

Kevin stepped over the coffee table and slid between us. "It's time for a break. Rocky, turn off the set."

Glancing at the television, I saw an Iranian student burning an American flag and a slight shiver ran down my back. They really hated us. Then the set turned black and I noticed the American flag plastered on the wall of the immaculate room where dust dared not dance.

Kevin placed a palm on my back and steered me toward the hallway. "How would you ladies like to take a tour of the quarters?"

Rocky grabbed Kevin by the shoulder. "Wait, New York, we can't take 'em back there."

Kevin shrugged the hand off. "So, who's going to say anything? We only give tours to girlfriends and good friends." Rocky shook his head in response.

Kevin pulled Ellen from the couch, and we started down the narrow hallway. There were three doors on each side. The only light came from the front room and back screen door. "The rooms are on either side with the shower and laundry room at the end." I turned to see Rocky tagging along behind us.

The last door on the right opened, and a thin Marine with a brown towel wrapped around his waist emerged. I'd seen him before playing spades at the pool and at the embassy theater. They called him Jeff.

His short, coarse, dark hair dripped water down his exposed, glistening, hairless torso. His shower shoes, dog tags, and the Saint

Christopher medal dangling from his neck played a strange melody as he headed towards us.

Kevin called out to him, "Mad Dog, put some clothes on, man."

With a bent head, Mad Dog ducked into the room on the right in front of us. His voice trailed behind him, "Screw you, New York." His door slammed shut.

Kevin shrugged. "You just witnessed the very white and very wet Mad Dog, Jeff." He raised his voice and spoke to Mad Dog's door, "He'd better come out here and mop up the water he dripped on the floor in case Gunny comes to inspect." The gunny sergeant was in charge of the Marines.

The pale, sick green color of the doors reflected off the shiny spotless floor—it was marred only by the small puddle in front of Mad Dog's door. Even that was soon gone, as he wordlessly opened the door and wiped it up with his Marine-issue brown towel.

The cold and naked walls were as gray as the floor. The only mark on any door was a dent about five feet six inches high, where something had been banged against the wood.

"Mad Dog lives with Doc," Kevin said. "Ronni, you've probably seen Doc at the tennis courts. He goes down there to watch the ladies in those short tennis skirts. Personally I think he'd have better luck if he lost the R.P.G., short for rape prevention glasses, the ugly black ones they issue in boot camp. Other than that, Doc studies for his officers' exam.

We stopped at the first set of doors, and Kevin pointed to the door across from Mad Dog's. "You ladies aren't really allowed back in the sleeping quarters—so keep it to yourselves. Otherwise Rocky and I may be thrown in the brig and never see the light of day."

"Not Rocky," Rocky reminded him. "New York, whose dumb idea this was."

Kevin ignored Rocky. "Across from Mad Dog and Doc are Killer and Ace. You rarely see Killer, but he's a good Marine to have around. When Mad Dog banged his head and split it open on the door, Killer stitched it up with his sewing kit."

"Oh, gross." I eyed the place the water puddle had been, imagining blood instead.

"You ladies might know Ace. He's the clown of the group. That's why he's Ace, like a card. We called him 'The Joker,' but he changed it to Ace. He thinks it's luckier. He claims the ladies always want to know why they call him Ace and he offers to let them find out, if you know what I mean?

"He and Doc are the only ones who went to college. I'm planning on going when I get stateside. Rocky, of course, is too stupid to attend."

"Shut up, New York," Rocky said.

I laughed, and spun around to watch Rocky turn redder.

"Anyway, Ace dropped out of junior college to become a Marine. His mom threw him out so he needed a place to go." *Maybe I wasn't the only one with a wicked mom.*

We moved on, following Kevin. When we came to the next set of doors facing each other across the hall, we stopped again.

"After Killer and Ace's room we get to Rocky and mine. Across from us is Voodoo." His voice dropped to a whisper. "I doubt you ladies have ever seen Voodoo."

"Why do you call him that?" I asked.

"Sh . . . sh," Kevin had his finger to his lips. "Strange things happen when he's around."

I understood and whispered, "Like what?"

"Sergeant Jefferson's tour of duty was up and Voodoo was his replacement. Of course we didn't call him Voodoo then. It was Corporal Peterson. Anyway, Sergeant Jefferson had the single room on account of him being the senior Marine. Killer wanted the single because he was senior after Doc, and Doc had pretty much settled in with Mad Dog and didn't want to move.

"Killer said living with Ace was cruel and unusual punishment. He packed up Voodoo's stuff and left it outside the door. Voodoo didn't say a word, like he didn't even notice. He didn't even unpack."

I looked at Ellen; she clung to Kevin's arm as if looking for protection. Rocky said, "Wo . . . o," in my ear as though he was a ghost.

I elbowed him in the ribs and turned to Kevin. "Go on. Then what happened?"

"That night, Killer was working on his abs when the cable on the machine snapped. He pulled a muscle in his back and had trouble moving for days. We thought it was a coincidence.

"But, the next day at mail call, a letter came addressed to Sergeant Henry—that's Killer. He took the mail to his room to read. Later, we thought we heard a noise like a muffled scream coming from the room. Ace put his ear to the door and reported it sounded like crying; but he had to be wrong because Marines don't cry. We have our code."

"So what was it?" I asked.

Kevin shook his head. "We never found out. It'll probably die with Killer."

"And that's it?" I asked. "Two things and the guy's marked as a jinx?" They were obviously making more out of a little coincidence.

"Sh!" Kevin put his finger to his lips and looked around as though the walls had eyes.

"Sorry," I whispered.

"No, there's more. Ace had to sleep two nights with Voodoo. He says he slept with one eye open all night. Ace is the one who gave Corporal Peterson the name Voodoo. Usually the person who knows you best gives you your nickname. Rocky gave me mine, 'New York,' on account of my accent and the little Statue of Liberty I got on my desk."

"Is that all?" I asked. "The whole story about," I lowered my voice, "Voodoo?"

"No." He spun around and clumped a hand on Rocky's shoulder. "You want to tell the rest?"

"You're doing fine," Rocky said.

Ellen leaned closer to him and nodded. "Okay," Kevin said. "Ace didn't give Voodoo his nickname until the fateful night he was imitating Voodoo's walk and laughing. Voodoo walked in. He didn't say anything. We weren't even sure that he understood what was going on. But that night Ace fell and bit his tongue clear through. It was swollen for a month.

"Nobody calls him Voodoo in his presence so don't let that slip when he's around. Ace says he is from New Orleans, but who knows?"

I felt a chill run down my spine, and the hallway seemed darker. Behind the closed door a scary guy might be practicing black magic that very moment. "Boo!" Rocky yelled in my ear. I jumped before turning around to punch him.

Rocky grabbed my wrist as Ellen and Kevin laughed.

"You're lying. You're just trying to scare me," I said.

"No, Marines don't lie," Kevin said. "It's the God-honest truth."

He opened the door to his room. I peered under his arm, eager to see what secrets hid within. "Rocky, go keep watch for Gunny in the common room."

"Yeah, yeah, yeah." Rocky left and we followed Kevin inside.

"No one's allowed back here except other Marines and I guess the coroner if one of us dies in our sleep. If Gunny found you two here, I'd be out a month's pay."

The room was about twelve by twelve feet. It was smaller than my room and it looked like no one lived in it. Bunk beds sat against one wall. Bars covered the window. The floor was naked, the type you'd hate to have to step onto with bare feet in the morning. There were no pictures of family, no football trophy or letterman jacket. No posters hinted at which movie actor or band the occupants preferred. Ellen moved closer to me and grabbed my arm.

Kevin pointed at the bunk bed. "I sleep on the top, Rocky on the bottom."

The room was a holding pen, a place to pass time. I saw a movie once in which prisoners carved their initials in the plaster wall. When Kevin was gone, would his initials hide somewhere in that room? Late at night, would the moon cast a shadow that resembled his profile? Or would he go without leaving a trace?

"The only thing that can be displayed under the beds are our combat boots," Kevin continued. "Mine at the foot. Rocky's at the head. His footlocker fits in between the boots. My footlocker's at the end of the bed. There's a padlock on each locker, but we never keep them locked—nothing in them to steal. Besides, Marines don't steal."

I started to lift the lid, but Kevin stopped me. "No, don't touch anything, Ronni. I can't have fingerprints on anything."

"Excuse me," I apologized but didn't know what the big deal was.

"That desk there by the window is Rocky's. That's the only place Gunny doesn't inspect. So we can keep our personal papers and things in there.

"Rocky won't tell you himself, but he has a dozen pictures of his twin sisters. They just turned nine. He also keeps all the artwork they send him. He has a picture of his mom at his graduation from basic training and another he ripped in half in order to get rid of the part with his stepfather. He also keeps a picture of his father in a plastic bag because it's faded and old. It must have been taken shortly before his dad split on him."

Suddenly, I felt sorry for Rocky. I remember he told me he missed his sisters the first night he heard me talking to Juma. I wanted to know more. Ellen must have read my thoughts because she asked, "Can we take a peek?"

"Sorry, maybe another time. That desk over there's mine. I keep plenty of family photos. I have four brothers and two sisters. Yeah, I know what you're thinking, big Catholic family. That's also where I keep the crucifix and the Statue of Liberty my mom sent me. The day that came, I got my name—New York. It wasn't like Ace hadn't been imitating my New York accent for weeks, but when my statue came my fate was sealed."

Ellen smiled and gave him a little kiss. He blushed and continued, "The rooms are pretty small, but we also have wall lockers for storage. Inside these lockers we keep our alpha and bravo blues. The difference between our alphas and bravos is on the alphas we wear our ribbons and badges, things we earn with qualifications and on the bravos our medals, which we earn for meritorious service, but no badges."

"Do you have any medals?" I asked.

"Yeah, a few," he said smiling at Ellen. "Anyway, those are our uniforms for duty. I have my lance corporal stripes. Lance corporal is one step up from corporal. Rank stripes are worn on the sleeve. When I have four years in, I get my first hash mark. You get one for every four. Rocky has one, but he's been in five years. He also ran away from home to enlist at seventeen. The idea was, he was going to learn seven ways to kill a man with his bare hands before going home and putting it into practice."

A door slammed in the hallway. "Hey Gunny!" Rocky yelled. "What's new?"

We heard the deep mumbled response. "Oh shit, Gunny," Kevin said.

Then Rocky continued in an unnaturally loud voice, "Yeah, just watching a little tube."

Another mumble.

"It's a terrible shame about those guys."

Kevin put his finger to his lips, moved the footlocker, and pointed under the bed. "Hide under there. Quick," he whispered.

Ellen slid under the bed and I crammed in after her. I felt an alarming sense of claustrophobia when Kevin replaced the footlocker to shield us from view.

I heard Kevin's feet padding towards the door.

"So, this is what their quarters look like," I whispered, trying to control my fear of suffocating stuck under the bed. "Small."

Ellen adjusted her legs to fit better. "It's okay. It's only temporary."

We heard footsteps and I ducked my head, afraid that Gunny would hear me exhale.

Through the door, it sounded like Kevin said, "Yeah, Gunny, those are real good men at that embassy. I hope they get freed soon."

The door creaked. I closed my eyes; afraid I'd go crazy and cry out. The bed pinned me down and I couldn't move. I shook my legs. I needed out, immediately. Ellen grabbed my hand and held it.

A pair of boots followed a pair of white socks across to the wall lockers.

"Corporal Carlson, open your wall locker," Gunny said. It was the first time I heard Kevin referred to by his last name and rank.

"Yes, Gunny," Kevin said, removing the lock.

The pair of boots paced back and forth, two steps to the left and then two to the right.

"Okay now, Sergeant Ross, yours."

Rocky opened his.

"Sergeant, yours could use some air freshener," Gunny said. "It's musty."

"Yes, Gunny. I'll get some right away."

"Corporal Carlson, your foot locker."

I opened my eyes. They came right at us. What if I jumped up and screamed? What if I couldn't stay pinned down any longer? Suddenly I needed to pee. The lid of the footlocker went up, making it impossible for me to see anything. I bit my tongue and clamped my legs together.

There was a rustle in the locker. Could they see me? I could push the lid down and Gunny would know. "How'd you get these to shine, son?" Gunny said. He must've been talking about the shoes.

"I heated up the wax and applied it while still hot." Who cared about his stupid shoes? I was going crazy. I curled my fingers and released them a dozen times. Kevin continued, "Then I used ice water." If I yelled, it would all be over. "And a cotton ball to rub it all in."

"Okay, just make sure you hide away your polish kit. It gives it an unsightly appearance." Maybe we could jump out and pretend Kevin didn't know we were there. The lid snapped shut. "What's that smell?" Could he smell fear?

"Wh—what smell Gunny?" Kevin asked, voice trembling.

"Probably just my locker, Gunny," Rocky offered.

"No, it smells like perfume. Where's it coming from?"

I knew Ellen wore Chanel and a lot of it. I bit my lip and she looked at me, eyes wide, fingers rapidly twirling a strand of hair. We were caught. Better give it up now. I fought the urge to push the footlocker by squeezing my eyes shut and shaking my leg.

"Ah . . . it's perfume," Kevin stammered. "Yeah, Gunny, do you like it? I bought some for my girl. I tested it. It's probably on the blanket. Sorry, Gunny, won't happen again."

"Wash it tonight." The boots turned toward the door, "Okay, Sergeant . . . Corporal, carry on."

The door closed and footsteps faded away. I shoved the footlocker, trying to free myself.

Someone shoved it back. "Wait a minute," Kevin warned. "I have to see if the coast's clear." He went off, returning after a minute to free us.

Afraid Gunny would return, Kevin shoved us out the screen door in the back. When Kevin closed the door behind us, Ellen turned to me and said, "He's so clever. I think I love him."

"Already?" When I saw the pained look on her face, I wished I could take it back. "I'm glad for you," I lied.

"He asked me to wear his ring." She put up her ring finger. "Hey, maybe you could date Rocky. That way we could double," Ellen said. Was that the way she kept her promise to put our friendship first? She'd make it fit to her satisfaction?

I pushed aside my anger and asked, "Do you think they'll let the hostages go in Iran?"

Chapter Twenty

When I got home, silence enveloped the house. Mom and Amy attended another one of Amy's soccer practices. I passed Rashid on the stairs to the second floor. "Where's my dad?" I asked.

"Sahib, in room. Very quiet. No loud," he warned me.

I needed to ask my father why people like Rashid's brother, Muhammed, hated us and what he thought might happen in Iran. There might not be a better time. Dragging my feet through the lawn of beige carpet, I passed the huge mahogany door shutting me out of my father's world. A soft glow creeping under the door provided the only hint of life.

My fingertips brushed the bumpy wall and I turned my head to look at that glow. *Would he be busy? Should I? Okay, I would.* Backing up cautiously, with an ear close to the door, I listened. There was the sound of a paper being turned. Since the hostage situation began he had hardly come out to eat and he was always in a bad mood.

I notice the door stood slightly ajar. He hadn't shut it all the way. Was it an invitation?

I pushed the door with one finger. It fought the burgundy carpet lining the study's floor, but creaked and opened a crack, then hung up, resisting my trespass. The light flickered like a hooded candle on his stone-like desk. I peered inside and saw my dad's sensible brown shoes rooting themselves to the thick rug. Hesitating only a moment, I knocked.

I heard a stifled cough and low growl before he said, "Come in." He sat slumped over the desk, bifocals perched halfway down his nose, a document clutched in the hand resting in his lap.

The desk spread out, covering half the room. Piles of papers in in-boxes, stone paperweights, and more documents crowded its surface. I could detect the faint odor of alcohol wipes and a splash of Old Spice aftershave as well as a musty library smell.

"I was just wondering," I said. "You know what happened at the embassy in Iran?" I waited and saw a slow nod of his head. "Well, could it happen here, too?"

He reached for a water glass under the lamp. After a deliberate sip he answered, "For reasons you're too young to understand, some students decided to hold those people hostage. They let ten of them go today. It'll all be over soon."

Wanting to believe him, I probed a little further. "I know they want the Shah back. But the U.S. was friends with Bhutto, too. Maybe they're mad at us."

His intake of breath was deeper. After a long time he exhaled, "No, it's a different situation. The U.S. has a different relationship with Zia's government here than we had with Iran." He pushed his glasses back up his nose and straightened the document in front of him. "We're safe," he said. "Go on now."

I bit my lip and asked, "Are you CIA?"

His eyes darted to mine and he stared at me over his bifocals. "What?" He looked away and rustled the paper. "You know I'm an agriculture attaché. I help with import and export of crops. Where did you come up with this CIA stuff?"

"I . . . I just thought because we left Morocco so quickly in the middle of the school year and you always read about Iran and Pakistan. Well, I just thought."

He turned back to his reading. "You don't need to worry. I'll tell you what you need to know."

It wasn't an answer, but I knew he wasn't allowed to give me one anyway. I picked my way cautiously but swiftly over the carpet, as though avoiding land mines. He hadn't been in Kabul and he hadn't seen how everything could seem just fine until it all blew up.

*   *   *

A few days later Ellen and I sat in the community room of the Marine quarters again, with Rocky and Kevin. Ace sat watching the television and ignoring us. Kevin shuffled a deck of cards. "We'll play to 500, okay?"

"Sure, whatever," I agreed.

"Ace, you want to play?" Rocky asked.

Ace slumped in the chair turned backward so his elbows rested on the top of the chair's back. He faced the television set, and he didn't turn his head, "Is it strip spades?"

Rocky threw a foam football at his head.

"Ouch. What?" Ace turned around rubbing his temple. "I'm just asking."

"You naked? Don't scare us, man," Rocky teased.

Ace turned back to the television. "Shut up, man, I'm trying to listen."

"It's in Urdu," Rocky said, glancing at the set. "Hey, that's Farmer." He pointed. "What do ya know? He's over there."

I stood and moved toward the set. Three people stood at the door to a plane. Two African American Marines in camouflage sandwiched a thirty-something woman with short brown hair.

"Are those the ones they're releasing?" I asked.

"Yeah, women and brothers," Rocky grunted. "So Killer'd get to go, but we'd have to stay."

In an attempt to see through the snowy reception the old set received, I moved closer. "Why?" I asked. "They're all Americans."

"I can't see through you," Ace barked. I jumped back.

"Well, the women—," Kevin explained, "for obvious reasons, and the brothers so the Iranians can show solidarity with their oppressed African brothers."

"What?" I asked.

"Come sit on my lap, Ronni, and I'll explain it to you," Rocky said with a smile.

"Shut up," I said. "Do you think they'll let them all go soon?"

"Ronni!" Kevin ignored the question. "You going to play or not?"

"Yeah. I just wanted to see."

"Admit it, you wanted to sit next to me." Rocky made room on the couch beside him.

"I'm sitting in the chair so I don't have to sit next to Rocky," I said. "He looks at my cards."

"Is anyone playing?" Kevin demanded.

I couldn't concentrate on anything but whether we were safe. I remembered the eyes of Rashid's brother, Muhammed. Dad said students took the hostages. What if the students in Pakistan hated us too?

Chapter Twenty-One

November 21, 1979, was the last day of school before the four-day Thanksgiving weekend. The weather started to get cold and I wore a windbreaker to keep out the chill.

Amy and Mom left with a bunch of sophomores on a field trip to see the Moenjodaro archaeological site. I didn't know whether to be jealous because Amy didn't have to go to school or relieved that I wouldn't have to put up with her for a few days.

After lunch, I had world history. Mrs. Cook's room was serious, with huge maps of China, India, Iran, Iraq, Afghanistan, and Pakistan, of course. Pieces of red, blue, and green yarn connected places with newspaper and magazine articles. Pictures of Chairman Mao Tse-tung with Richard Nixon, the Shah Mohammad Reza Pahlavi, the Ayatollah Khomeini, Gandhi, Bhutto, and more plastered the wall.

The most haunting of the pictures was the newest; of five blindfolded hostages photographed on November 10. One wore a short-sleeve brown Marine uniform shirt, with a black nametag over the left pocket and service ribbons over his heart. His undershirt showed. The other four wore jeans and t-shirts. I wondered if they would have dressed differently if they'd known they wouldn't be able to change for a while.

The bookshelf lining the front wall bustled with globes and World Book and other encyclopedias. That room never saw a wasted hour, even on the day before the Thanksgiving holiday.

"Your report on Southeast Asia should be at least 500 words long," Mrs. Cook said. "Since you have a long weekend you will have plenty of time to finish it."

A collective groan sounded around the classroom. The clock above the exit read 12:45. A sharp rap sounded at the door.

Mr. Kain, our assistant principal, opened it and motioned to Mrs. Cook. The two huddled in the doorway whispering, too low for me to eavesdrop.

In a moment, Mrs. Cook turned to the class and said, "Excuse me for a minute. I have to step out; you start your assignment. I'll check your progress when I return."

Once the door closed, the volume in the room began to rise. Danny East ran around with a meter stick balanced on his lower lip. Ellen, who shared World History with me, but no other classes because she was a senior, jumped up and guarded the door right next to my desk.

Ian pushed his desk up against mine "I could really use a cig," he said.

"Don't even think about it," I replied. "Cook'll smell it. She'll be back any second. Let's just start the essay, okay?"

"Okay, brain, what do we write?"

"Shut up, Ian. I'm not a brain. I just don't want to spend my weekend doing the essay."

"So, you got a big weekend planned? Who's the guy?"

"No one . . . I'm having Thanksgiving at home, sleeping in Friday morning and watching Friday night's *The Six Million Dollar Man*."

On Friday nights, every English-speaking person in Islamabad stopped what they were doing to watch the only television program broadcast in English, reruns of *The Six Million Dollar Man*. "I just don't want to work over the weekend and we have to be here right now anyway, so why not?"

Another classmate, Tracy, visited the pencil sharpener, and then stood five paces behind my desk, as though waiting to be told what to do next. Her large eyes shifted behind her spectacles and sweat plastered her short hair against her scalp.

"Well." I flipped through my notes. "Should we start when Pakistan was part of India?"

Ian leaned close to my ear and said, "I think I love you."

I drew back in surprise. "What?" I flicked my wrist at him. "Shut up, Ian. Get serious." He didn't respond, but looked a little hurt, so I added, "Come on, let's just do this." His gaze burned into my face as I looked away. My stomach tickled and I felt scared. I cared about Ian, but if I let him know that, then what? I couldn't go back on it if he changed his mind.

"That's a lot of information to cover." Ellen leaned over towards my desk. "And we do have six other countries."

"It only been thirty-one years since India was split into two countries," I argued.

"Should we write that down?" Tracy asked.

"I'm going to start with hostages taken in Iran," Luke said from across the room.

Rebecca, the Canadian Ambassador's daughter, reminded him, "This isn't a paper on the United States, and it has to be at least 500 words."

"I think we should date," Ian whispered, leaning next to my ear again.

"What? Ian, be real."

"Why not? We're friends. Remember when we first met, you had that half heart around your neck?" I nodded as he touched my Sihk bracelet and gently twirled it around with his fingers. The warmth of his skin brushed my wrist. "I've thought about how to steal your heart ever since."

I wondered how many times he had said similar things to other girls. I took my hand away from his. "If we went out, we wouldn't be friends anymore."

Ian looked away; I followed his gaze to Danny, who shoved pencils up his nose. "Man, aren't you going to do your essay?" Ian asked Danny.

Danny shrugged and made a stupid face. No one laughed.

I leafed through my notes. I read over the part where Pakistan got its name from all the Muslim providences: *P for Punjab, A for Afghans, K for Kahmir, S for Sind and then the 'istan' for the Urdu word 'Land of.' Put together, it is Pakistan, meaning 'Land of the Pure.'* It was like poetry. "Maybe we should mention how Pakistan and India split due to religious differences? We might emphasize Pakistan and the Muslims. What do you think?"

Tracy sat with her pencil poised. "Should we write that?" She shoved her glasses back up her nose. "Where is it in our notes?"

"Ronni, write it for me," Ellen said.

"I'm only a junior. You're the senior in this class. You should write my paper," I teased her.

"I'm writing about the Hindus," Ranjit, from India, said. "We, too, have a long history of civil war with Pakistan. I think we should mention Gandhi."

"Who cares?" Ellen argued. "This isn't a religion paper."

I hesitated, and, despite the fact that my next thought could be construed as geek-like, I proceeded. "I think all countries fight about religion. In fact, religion seems to be the only reason they hate each other. Religious politics." I looked around for agreement and was met with silence. "Right?" I stammered.

The eerie quiet ended when Tracy asked, "Should we write that?"

Ian, Ellen, and I laughed. "Ronni, write my paper for me," Ian said.

"Forget you."

"Does that mean we're through?" he asked.

I smiled at him. "We never began."

Ellen leafed through her notes and started summarizing. "India was divided into three sections: West Pakistan, India, and East Pakistan and then East Pakistan became the new nation of Bangladesh. China is a communist country under Chairman Mao. What about Iran and Iraq? The Soviets invaded Afghanistan. Anything else?"

"Are you going to write that?" Tracy nudged me.

Ian laughed. "Let's all just take a different country, get some facts and share them."

"Our papers can't all be the same," Ellen said.

Suddenly a paper airplane bounced off my head and fell on my desk. The word "dumb" was scrawled on it. I looked around the room and saw a dozen airplanes on Luke's desk.

Ian grabbed the airplane, leapt onto his desk, balled it up and chucked it forcefully at Luke's head. Danny dove right into the paper fight.

I rescued my notes and moved away from the action. Lifting my folder and ducking, I avoided a paper ball, which bounced off my binder and hit Tracy. She didn't seem to notice as she shook, wringing her hands. "What should we write?" She whined. "We'll get in trouble if Mrs. Cook walks in."

Just as she said that, Danny got a permanent black marker from Mrs. Cook's desk and went toward the displayed pictures.

"Ian, make him stop!" I yelled. "He'll draw a mustache on Chairman Mao!"

Ian dove off the desk and tackled Danny, taking him down to the ground. "My nose!" Danny yelled. "You're crushing me. Get off!"

"Not until you hand over the marker, man."

Luke entered the struggle, gave Danny an elbow to the back, and sat on his legs. Ian held up the marker as if it were the Olympic torch.

Danny struggled to his feet and emptied the trashcan onto Luke's head. Ian jumped in between the two boys. "I'm going to kill you!" Luke threatened.

Ian prevented the murder by snatching up about ten paper balls and sharing them with Luke. They both pounded Danny. Ranjit got hit and joined in the fight.

Minutes later, Ellen sounded the alarm. "Someone's coming!"

There was a huge scramble to pick up paper and other trash. Danny struggled to get a pencil eraser out of his nose.

I pushed the desks back in order, while Tracy got in my way, trembling so hard, she seemed to have forgotten where she sat. "I didn't write anything. What if she checks? Did you write anything, Ronni?"

"Stop worrying. Go sit down. If she asks tell her, you need more time. Hurry."

The door opened as I slid into my desk. I sunk down low in the seat, hoping Mrs. Cook would believe Danny's nose had spontaneously started bleeding, and that she had left her black marker on the floor. No one said a word, but everyone pretended to be totally engrossed in the blank pages that were supposed to be our essays.

Mrs. Cook looked flushed and her hand trembled as she picked up the marker. "What's up, Ms. C?" Ian said, breaking the silence. "Talk to me."

The words seemed to come from her nose, "Well . . . there appears to be a civil disturbance. The American Embassy is involved."

Everyone talked at once. I knew it. They had taken hostages. My father had been wrong, and now he was probably being blindfolded and there was nothing I could do.

"Wait, wait, class. We don't know all the facts yet. After sixth period, we hope we'll be able to tell you more."

"What? No way, man," someone yelled. "I can't wait. My dad's in there."

Tracy turned a paler shade of ivory and whispered, "Can I go to the nurse?" Her father worked as an engineer and wasn't even associated with the American Embassy.

"Let's just cancel school and go home," someone suggested.

Danny agreed. "Yeah, let's go home."

A chant began, "Let's go home! Let's go home!"

Mrs. C. stopped that. "If you have so much time on your hands, maybe we'll make it an 800-word report."

To my relief, the bell rang. We entered the hall where more pandemonium raged. Coach Campbell attempted to head off the confusion by standing in the center of the hallway and, in a voice that seemed to break through all conversation, repeated, "It's all over! Get to class! Nothing to worry about. The whole thing has blown over. Move it!"

I waved goodbye to Ellen, wondering how honest Coach was being. I took off for science. It was my last period, and I had it with Mr. Malone, the human gorilla. He had told the class a story about how, one summer at the Holiday Inn, a kid ran from the pool screaming, "Mom, it's an ape!" He claimed to have tons of back and chest hair and, after seeing the fur that stuck out the collar of his shirt, we just took his word for it.

Like every other day, we took out our science labs to turn in without even being told and sat to copy the assignment off the board. While Mr. Malone took roll, Danny dared to send spitballs flying into Rebecca and Tracy's hair. He was about to let loose another barrage when Mr. Malone hurled an eraser at his head. It hit Danny smack on the left cheek.

For about twenty seconds, no one spoke. We sat paralyzed with disbelief, until Rebecca started to giggle, and Ian boldly let out a full, hardy laugh. But Mr. M. didn't crack a smile and in a moment, we all stared directly at our science notes again. Mr. Malone was allowed a certain leeway because he was a widower with a young son. No one knew how Mrs. Malone died. For all we knew, he had killed her.

A minute later, a knock sounded at the door. Mr. Malone poked his head out, and then stepped all the way out, leaving the door open no more than a crack.

Ian bravely took out his pack of Camels and tapped them on the desk. I glared at him as he pretended to offer me one. I grabbed his hand. "Put it away."

"Aw, if I smoke one, you wanta kiss me?" He puckered up his full lips.

I smiled, shaking my head. Despite myself, I felt a tingle in my stomach. No, I couldn't let him know how much I wished he'd kiss me.

Mr. Malone peered back in and Ian slid the cigarettes under his desk.

"I'm going to be in the office for five minutes." He held out the fingers on one hand to emphasize the time. "Open your books to page thirty-five. Read and answer the questions. I want them finished in complete sentences by the end of class." The door closed with a thud.

"Not again," Rebecca moaned.

"Do you think our dads are safe?" I whispered to Ian.

He smiled and put a hand on my cheek. "They'll be fine."

Everyone looked at Danny to see if he was going fool around. He peered back at us over the top of his book, smirking. "You think he'll be back?" Danny asked.

"What if it's something serious?" Tracy whimpered. "What are we going to do?"

Ian stood up. "We don't know what's going on." He walked down the aisle and put a hand on Tracy's shoulder. "All we have to do is wait to go home."

Half an hour later, Mr. Fox, a sixth-grade teacher, opened our door. Danny, one hand in the air about to let fly an eraser, dropped back in his seat.

"Okay, everyone in the auditorium. Let's go," Mr. Fox ordered.

"Can't we just go home? It's the last day of school. I want to go to the office to call home. My mom'll pick me up," everyone complained.

"Can we do that?" Tracy whispered to me.

I shrugged. We all got up and made our way to the auditorium with a flood of questions and comments.

The whole school crammed in there, from kindergarten to seniors. Three sections of staggered seats fanned out in the room and in the aisle large concrete steps led to the polished, wooden stage up front. The teachers stood guard over us in the aisles, shushing everyone with weak, "Sh . . . sh . . . ," sounds and fingers to their lips. I searched the crowd for

Ellen but Mr. Fox ordered me to sit before I could find her among the seniors.

A few parents entered the auditorium and, with the help of teachers, started pulling their kids out to take them home. That's when it hit me. My dad—where was he? He usually got off at six, and Mom and Amy were in Moenjodaro. Wouldn't Dad be at the school already if he was okay? Maybe he thought I'd just catch the school bus.

Mr. Kain walked to the center of the stage and tapped the microphone, which squawked. "Okay, settle down, everyone." Mr. Kain raised his hand like a crossing guard.

"Students, the buses won't be running today," Mr. Kain said.

What did he say? No way! A moan enveloped the room. How would I get home?

"Quiet now. I have an announcement. There is a demonstration and we can't risk running the buses."

"It's our vacation. Come on, man." Several fists rose into the air.

Some brave souls agreed loudly in unison, "Yeah!"

"Let's go. I got a car," a senior boy said, standing as if to leave until Mrs. Campbell went over to stand behind him and he quickly sat.

"Give me a ride," another pleaded.

Peals of laughter echoed through the room. Mr. Fox pulled Danny aside for putting a "kick me" sign on Stacy's back and over his shoulder, I saw Ellen two rows back to my left; I waved. She waved back, pointing a finger at me to indicate she'd join me.

Frowning deeply, Mr. Kain continued, "You have to wait for your parents to pick you up."

It dawned on me that I might not be picked up. *Would my father even remember me? I might be here until midnight—all-alone.* The

O'Malley's lived on Nara, too, but they rode the bus. Would their mother come? Or would I have to bum a ride from a senior?

"We're going to watch a movie."

"*North Dallas Forty*," someone yelled. The crowd laughed.

"*Rocky Two*," another voice yelled.

"Yeah, *Rocky* rules," someone agreed. A few whistles followed.

Ian slid down in his seat, made his voice higher and yelled, "*The Muppet Show*." Everyone stared at me.

"No way!" Danny yelled at me.

"I didn't say it! I didn't! Damn you, Ian!" I punched him.

He grabbed my hand. "Oh, Ronni." I pulled it back.

Mr. Kain shook his head and said, "Students. Now . . ." He cleared his throat and pointed towards Mrs. Cook who flipped the light switch.

We never saw any recent movies, and that day was no different. Mr. Rhoads, Ellen's father, threaded the 1950's 8mm film of *U.S. Rodeos* through the machine.

We sounded our collective groan of displeasure and Rebecca and Luke asked Mr. Fox to be excused to visit their lockers. The faint light of the late afternoon continued to invade the room as more people left and others returned.

Ian's brother Edward came by to bum a cig off Ian. They went for the door with Edward's friend Jaime in tow.

Ellen plopped into the seat beside me and grabbed my arm. "Oh, Ronni. There's something going on at the embassy. A riot or something. Kevin's on duty."

"A riot? What about the people who work there? We'd hear if something bad happened, wouldn't we? Besides they have the gate and a lock for the door. Nothing's going to happen to 'em."

But the embassy in Iran had been attacked and the gate hadn't stopped the mob. If Dad couldn't get out, I'd be stranded at school forever. At least Mom and Amy traveled safely to Moenjodaro, but what if rioters attacked their train or the school?

About twenty minutes later, in a rush and a breath of smoke, Ian and Edward shoved their way down the row to us.

"Man, Ronni, the embassy's on fire."

"What?" Ellen said, grasping my hand. "Kevin!"

"What do you mean?" *Where was my Dad?*

"We saw it. You can see it from over the top of the library. Plus, some French guy bummed a cig . . ." He hauled in a breath and coughed. "The guy says he thinks everyone may be dead."

Ellen's grip got tighter on my hand. I felt nothing else for a few seconds.

Then a familiar sting rose in my eyes. My dad might be dead. When I was seven I had seen the movie, *I Never Danced for My Father*, and I couldn't stop crying afterwards. I couldn't imagine losing my father. I had changed since then; now I didn't cry easily. I didn't want to think about my dad. He'd shown me the world and I was too ungrateful to appreciate him. And now, now he might be gone, once again changing my life forever.

Ellen cried, able to express the emotion I refused to as I prayed silently, "please God don't let anything happen to my dad."

As though I were miles away, standing outside myself, I heard my words, "It's okay, Ellen. It's going to be okay."

The lights came on, and Mr. Kain spoke again, "We're all moving to the gym. Let's go. And don't stop by your lockers. You'll be allowed to do that later."

Ian asked, "You okay, Ronni?"

I tried to smile at him, but then the tears started. He flung his arm around me, and I sobbed into his t-shirt. I didn't even mind the smoky odor. He kissed my hair and whispered, "It's okay," in my ear.

After a moment, I pulled back and clutched Ellen. "I'm fine. Really, it's nothing. It's just my dad; he's in there . . . I can't get home now."

Ellen hugged me and, we both cried some more. Ian circled us with his arms. Afterwards, sniffling, we moved along with the tail end of the crowd heading for the gym.

Inside, Coach Campbell passed out footballs and basketballs. Ian took one while Ellen and I sat on the cold concrete blocks that led to the basketball court.

A few minutes later, Wendy Chapman, a third-grader, ran in to the gym screaming. "They're here! They're coming to get us!"

Coach Campbell grabbed her and pulled her into a corner. In a moment, he yelled, "Clear out. Everyone find a place to hide. Move quickly!"

People scattered in every direction. Edward and Jaime ran under the shamiana, the brown canvas curtain, separating the gym from the cafeteria. Ellen grabbed my arm and spun me around toward the girls' locker room. We dashed through the door, which closed behind us.

Students crouched, sat, and stood in showers, restroom stalls, and under benches. Some crammed in the lockers. There was no room for us. Ellen pulled me out and jammed me into a broom closet. She slammed the door and we huddled in darkness holding our breaths.

I heard loud voices, objects smashing, glass breaking, and a bang like a gun. Ellen clutched my head. I prayed in a whisper, "Oh, my God, oh, my God."

After a few minutes it was silent. Then I heard footsteps.

The lock of the door clicked and the door opened. Ellen buried her face in my shoulder and we huddled closer together. The door opened. Angry dark eyes stared down at us. I recognized the hostile face of Muhammed, Rashid's brother. I remembered how he had told us to get out of his house. Fear paralyzed me. I couldn't speak, couldn't plead for my life.

Muhammed yelled in Arabic. Was he calling the others to attack us? I heard feet running, coming closer. I stepped in front of Ellen; my eyes pleaded with Muhammed's for a moment.

Then, before the other attackers arrived, Muhammed said something and slammed the door shut on us.

Was he trapping us in? What did he intend to do? What should we do?

Footsteps retreated from the door and disappeared. Ellen whimpered, "What happened?"

"I don't know." *Why would he let us go?*

We sagged to the floor and sat in the dark for what felt like hours until we heard Mr. Fox's voice. "Is anyone in there?" he shouted. "You can come out now! It's over. They're gone."

Laughter erupted in my throat for no reason. Ellen and I tumbled out of the closet and ran back into the gym.

The shamiana had been ripped down and glass covered the cafeteria floor. A chair lay on its side in the middle of the mess.

Ian supported Edward, who had his windbreaker wrapped around his left hand. Jaime held him up on the other side. Edward's face screwed up in pain.

"What happened?" I asked, pulling Ellen over to the boys.

Edward talked quickly, "Jaime and I were hiding under the shamiana. Surrounded by boxes. Five or six Pakistani guys came in. One had a shotgun and we heard a bang. They threw chairs. One broke through the window of the cafeteria."

"Did they see you?" I asked.

"They must have. I ran and tripped over the cooler and landed on my hand." He flinched and continued, "We could have made it out the back and across the field, but Wendy couldn't make it and we didn't want to leave her, so we hid in the locker room."

"Who were they?" I asked.

Mr. Fox joined us. "As far as we can tell, a busload of students from the local university. Now, we need to regroup in the music room. Let's go."

The trek to the music room took us from one quad to another. Outside, several native school aides ambled about armed with hockey sticks and baseball bats. I stopped, not knowing whether to run for my life or keep walking. Ellen and the others hesitated, too. Mr. Fox assured us, "No, they're the good guys. They helped chase away the bad guys by using the sports equipment."

Beyond the aides, near the front of the school, stood a few native soldiers.

"The military's here, too?" Ellen asked.

"It is an international school with ambassadors' kids from all embassies. They couldn't afford not to be."

Once in the music room, teachers counted and grouped us, as students shuffled in and out leaving with parents or returning from a locker.

Ellen's mom asked for volunteers to go search the auditorium for hidden students. Ellen's hand shot into the air and she grabbed mine to hold up.

"You did hear that one of them had a shotgun, right?"

Her eyes became misty and her lip trembled. I understood her need to take some action. We had no way of knowing what was happening at the embassy.

In the auditorium, we switched on the lights and called, "Anyone in here? The coast is clear."

There was no response, so we went onto the stage area. I pushed back the heavy green curtains. Dust floated into my nose and eyes. "Yuck."

Backstage, canvas cutouts of scenery and cardboard signs surrounded the piano. Boxes overflowed with props. The boxes were big enough to hide in. I peered inside them.

They held memories—many years of memories. One contained a few trophies and a picture. I grabbed the picture and dusted off the glass. The year was printed at the bottom, 1976. It was taken at the brick wall behind the soccer field—the whole school stuffed into one 8x10. The faces were too small to make out well, but I searched and found Frana, Alex, Matt, and Shawnee.

"Look, Ellen, there's Frana. You didn't know her. She's from Iran. I think you would have liked her. There's Shawnee Bhutto and Matt. And Alex, my dad says he has to learn to walk and talk again since the accident I told you about." I pushed away the thought of how Shawnee had lost his father—I was afraid to think about losing my own.

I handed her the picture. She took it. "They look so young," she said, squinting at the photo. "Did we ever look that young?"

The door to the auditorium opened, breaking the tomblike silence around us. Luke walked in. Ellen and I stared at him intently.

"I just left my jacket. My mom's here. I'm leaving."

"Does she have any news?" Ellen asked.

"She heard one Marine got shot."

Kevin? I looked at Ellen automatically.

"Shot?" She dropped the picture. It bounced once on the stage before landing face down and smashing into pieces. It felt like some kind of omen. I tried to shake off my dread, to be positive for Ellen's sake.

"There are eight Marines. It couldn't be Kevin. What are the odds?" I smiled. "I bet it was Rocky trying to be tough, showing off. He shot himself in the foot. They're probably laughing about it right now."

Ellen squinted at me and smiled, a smile that slid off her mouth as soon as it got there. "Yeah, sure it's not him. It can't be. It's someone else, not Kevin."

Luke picked up his jacket. "Got to go."

"There doesn't seem to be anyone here," I said, and we followed him out.

Luke's mom sat in the passenger seat beside a burly driver; Luke's brother sat in the back.

"Come on, Luke, hurry. It's getting dark," his mom complained. "It's bad enough out there."

"Hi, Mrs. Datan," I said, leaning in the passenger's side.

"Hi girls, are you going home soon? The streets are still full of protesters. I had to cover my head so I would look like a native to get here in one piece."

"Mrs. Datan, my dad is in the embassy and we," I pointed to Ellen, "have friends there. We want to know if they're okay. What have you heard?"

"Ambassador Hummel says that a Marine got shot in the head, and the rest are still trapped up in the third-floor vault. But they can't stay there much longer. The building's on fire. Are you girls going to be okay?"

Ellen nodded her head. I shrugged. "I don't know." In the sound of the muffler, my response was lost.

When the car disappeared around the corner, Ellen and I hurried back to the music room. My watch read five o'clock.

When we got there, only about forty students remained with the teachers.

Mrs. Rhoads pulled Ellen and me to the side, "Honey," she said to Ellen, "the embassy compound has been burned down. Everything we own is gone." Ellen started to weep softly and I put my arm around her shoulder. Mrs. Rhoads continued, "We don't know if anyone died there yet. The Millers also lived in the compound. So the teachers decided that the Millers will go home with you, Ronni. At least until we know about—"

"My dad?" I asked.

She looked down at the ground. "Coach Campbell offered to drive you home."

Was she keeping something from me? "What about my dad?"

"They're still in the embassy."

I bit my lip. "But, it's on fire."

"We know, Ronni, and I'm not going to lie to you. They may or may not be okay."

Bullets and fire—how was he supposed to be safe in that? "Thank you for telling me the truth." I didn't know what else to say.

I let go of Ellen and got into the back of the van. Coach Campbell asked us to put jackets over our heads and bend down but before I could do that, I had to talk to Ellen.

I rolled down the window. "It's going to be okay. They'll get out."

We each forced a smile. I grabbed her hand and held it. "Call me," she said.

I nodded. "See you Monday. Happy Thanksgiving."

The van started up and my hand slipped away from hers. I waved until Ellen got too small to see. *Where would she go? She had no house, nothing left. Maybe not even Kevin. Then it hit me, how could I call her?*

Was my father still alive? What about the rest of my family? If my family made it through this, I promised to be a better daughter.

Chapter Twenty-Two

The oldest Miller daughter, Jenny, rubbed her little sister's brunette hair as eight-year-old Susie cried all the way home. The middle daughter's brown eyes stayed focused on the dark sky as tears welled up and spilled over onto her pale cheeks. They lost their home, dog, everything.

Mrs. Miller's hair poked out at odd angles while leaves stuck in the strands. Her skirt was ripped, her panty hose torn, and the heel of one shoe was missing. "I was sitting in the American Club." Her hand shook as she reached for a cigarette. "Pakistani men broke into the club and yelled at us."

"Did you see the embassy? Did you see the fire? How about the guns? Did they shoot at you?" *She got out, but where was my dad?*

"The embassy and compound were on fire. We huddled at the concrete parking lot wall." She flicked her lighter and the flame trembled. "They spat and threw stones at us. Then they tried to force us on a bus. We resisted."

The van pulled up to my house. Akbar and Rashid waited with dinner for two. They had heard about the embassy attack, but they didn't know what Sahib wanted them to do.

The phone rang moments after we entered the house. I went for it, but Mrs. Miller stopped me. "No, Ronni, let me get it."

"Why? It's my phone." I grabbed for it but Mrs. Miller snatched it from me. "I had it." I hovered by the phone glaring at her. I hoped to hear my dad's voice.

She put her finger to her lips. "Sh." Then she talked into the phone. "Thank you . . . yes we understand . . . we will. Good night."

She turned to me. "They got out." *My dad was safe.* "They're at the British Embassy."

"When will he come home and what about the Marine?"

"The Marine died of a gunshot wound to the head. My husband and your dad will call as soon as they can."

"Which Marine?" I bit my lip waiting. *Please don't let it be Kevin or Rocky.*

"The newest one, Corporal Carlson."

My mouth hung open a few seconds before I could find the words, "Kevin?" I shook my head. "No, not Kevin. He can't be dead. He's going to marry Ellen. He can't die." I reached for the phone. "I have to call her."

Mrs. Miller pressed down on the phone. "Ronni, don't. We have to leave the line free for any news of your father and my husband."

"But I have to call Ellen. Kevin's dead. She needs to know." *What would I say to her?*

"I'm sure they'll tell her. We still don't know about the field trip or anything. No calls out and that's final."

"This isn't even your house," I said without thinking.

"No, mine burnt down. Aren't you glad you still have one?"

I remembered then that Ellen didn't have a house either. I couldn't call her.

No one I knew well had ever died. Well, my grandparents had, but I was very young and didn't really know them. Kevin was different. Two days ago, he was smiling and dealing a deck of cards. Losing him took away that safe feeling that nothing could shake my world. Losing Kevin made me numb and cold.

The clock in the living room read 6:57 when Dad walked through the door with Mr. Miller. They brought with them an overwhelming stench of smoke, and black ash stained their solemn faces and the soiled, rumpled clothing they wore.

The Miller girls ran to their father with hugs and tears.

"The house," they said. "Our puppy."

"I know," he answered.

My eyes met my dad's in an uncertain waltz. I looked down at his shirt, and spotted blood on the front of it. "Did . . . did you get hurt?" I asked.

He glanced down at the front of his shirt, touched the blood slowly and then met my eyes again.

"It's the Marine's."

Kevin's? My dad saw Kevin die.

His eyes filled with tears. Then I felt mine fill as well.

I put my hand on his arm. "I know he's dead," I said. "Kevin's dead."

That's when my dad put his arms around me and I sobbed. Poor Ellen, she'd lost the one she loved. I'd almost lost my family. There was no place safe, no guarantees, no sure things.

He pulled away after a while. "I have to call about your mother."

"I know," I said, wiping away a tear.

He shuffled up the stairs. I waited until he turned the bend of the staircase and trudged after him. He left the door open as though he knew I'd follow, and it would be easier on both of us for him to tell me that way. I listened while he dialed several numbers and identified himself. "I'm looking for my wife. Yes, they told me the students would be at the Lahore consulate. Yes, I'll hold."

"Judith?" He paused. "Yes, I'm okay . . . The attack started about one o'clock. They knocked down the gate. The Marines held them off as long as they could, but they broke down the front door. They used tear gas. We all headed for the third-floor vault and then the fire started . . ."

"We just got out. We were at the British Embassy. A few people had to be treated for smoke inhalation. I'm surprised more didn't die . . ."

"Yes, a Marine . . . Shot in the head."

"Do you want to talk to her?" I moved away from the shadow of the door and stood in the doorframe.

"Sure. Hold on." He held out the phone. "Ronni," he whispered as I moved forward and took it. "Your mom."

"Hi, Mom."

"So you had a little excitement at school today?"

"Yeah, Kevin got shot. He . . . He didn't. He didn't—" The words "make it" or "he died" stuck in my throat. But, that was it; he was gone.

"Who's Kevin?"

"The Marine. He died." I bit my lip. I wouldn't cry even though my eyes stung, not now.

"Well, at least you guys are okay."

"Yeah, but Ellen. She's my friend and they were—"

"I'm sorry, honey. We were really scared something bad happened to you guys. This call is costing a fortune. I need to get off the phone."

"Yeah," I whispered. *How dumb I was, thinking that over the miles the phone line would bring us together, that we could connect.*

"Love you," she said. "Now put your dad on."

"Me, too. Bye." *But I didn't, not then; maybe I didn't really love her at all. Maybe we just spoke the words we thought we were supposed to, like actors learning our parts.*

I handed my dad the phone and left the room. I closed the door on my way out.

*   *   *

"No!" I heard myself yell and realized I'd had a nightmare. Sweat covered my face. I wiped it with the sheet. Stillness filled the dark room. *Did I yell out loud? Maybe not, Jenny Miller didn't stir but remained curled up in the sleeping bag on the floor.* The clock across the room read two a.m.

A dim light crept under my door. The house should have been dark. I got up to investigate.

Opening the door, I noticed a distant light coming from the living room at the foot of the stairs. Someone had forgotten to turn a light off downstairs. Mom would have been upset at the wastefulness. I had to turn it off.

As I rounded the curve of the staircase, I heard voices. The adults. I skipped over the step that always gave me away with its groan and crept to the bottom silently. I scuttled along the wall to a spot outside the living room.

"—burned all around us," Mr. Miller said. "The mob screamed and shot through the air conditioning vents. The Marines saved our lives."

"I can't believe they let that young Marine just lie there in the vault to die," Mrs. Miller said. "Why?" *They let Kevin die. He must have been in such pain as he bled to death.* A shiver ran down my spine.

"We couldn't get out. They just broke down the gate," my dad explained. "We called for help with the radio equipment. Ambassador Hummel kept telling us help was on the way but it never . . ." After a short pause, his voice trembled as he continued, "They never did."

Mr. Miller took over. "The carpet caught fire and the tile started to buckle. We had to breathe through wet paper towels. We nearly died in there. It was close."

I heard a glass being placed on a hard surface. My dad cleared his throat. "We didn't know if they were still on the roof, but we had to get out of there. So, Sergeant Ross stuck his head out." Dad paused again.

I held my breath. Rocky stuck his head out even after an angry crowd had shot through the air-conditioning vents. He'd risked his own life even after Kevin had been shot.

Dad's voice shook as he went on, "He told us the coast was clear, and then he led us across the roof, apologizing for the smoke."

My eyes filled with tears, as I understood. Rocky was a Marine. He did what Marines do. I'd never been brave like that. I needed to do something. I needed to do what I could to help Ellen or Rocky.

Chapter Twenty-Three

The next day, Thanksgiving, I reached for the phone several times to call Ellen. Each time I remembered that I didn't know where she was.

Our Thanksgiving feast sat on the table: ham, meatloaf, hen, mashed potatoes, cranberry sauce, stuffing, biscuits, peas with onions and beets. Rashid bustled around placing paper napkins and china plates on the table. Mom's yellow and red place settings and napkin holders were missing, but the rest looked the same as it had every year in every country, but this year Mom and Amy were missing.

Usually, there had been at least a dozen people in the house. This meant we had two tables: one for adults and another for children. I'd always sat at the children's table, a card table. This year we all fit fine at the dining room table.

The adults sat at one end and drank their wine while we kids sat, silently at the other. The adult's talk centered around the fact that without an embassy, our fathers had no work place and without an embassy compound, the Millers had no home. Then it dawned on me, what happened to the Marine quarters.

"Where are the Marines sleeping?" I asked.

Mrs. and Mr. Millers' heads spun to stare at me. Dad studied me.

"What?"

I swiped my rough napkin over my mouth once. "There's no compound, so, where are the Marines sleeping?"

"I don't know." Mrs. Miller laughed like the question was absurd.

I glared at her. "And are they having Thanksgiving?"

Little Susie Miller, perhaps sensing the tension, started to weep softly. The adults looked at me with the same affection one might hold for mold. After hugging her youngest daughter, Mr. Miller raised his wine glass. "I'm sure they're eating a great Thanksgiving feast like this one. To great Thanksgivings and good friends and family to share them with." The adults all drank to that. The speech came easily when you had food to eat and you hadn't lost a good friend.

"How do you know?" I asked.

My dad's eyes narrowed. He leaned forward and his voice grew lower and threatening, "Ronni, you're interrupting."

I stabbed at a piece of dry turkey. "Well, I was just wondering why no one is concerned about the men who risked their lives and lost one of their friends—my friend, too, and their home. That's all." I stopped to blink back a tear. "Does anyone care? I can't even use the phone to see how my friends are." I broke it off. I refused to let them see me cry.

"Ronni, settle down. You're being rude," Dad warned me. "We're all upset. The Marines are being cared for like everyone else. Now let's finish this fine meal and stop this nonsense."

Just then the phone rang. Dad pointed a finger toward me as a warning not to make a move for it. He wiped his lips, excused himself, and went to answer the phone.

The littlest Miller girl had begun crying again and I felt like an intruder at my own dining room table. Rashid saved me when he came out from the kitchen to ask everyone if they wanted more water.

Dad came back. "That was Bob Thorton. We'll be leaving early tomorrow morning."

"What?" Everyone spoke at once. "Where? Leaving? How long? What about . . . ?"

"Quiet, let him finish," Mr. Miller said.

"We're going back to Washington," Dad explained.

"Huh?" I asked.

Dad stood at the head of the table. "We pack one suitcase each. A few people will stay behind, but the majority of us are being evacuated."

"No way." I got up and glared at him. We weren't leaving, not again, not so soon.

"Ronni, sit down." I hesitated a few minutes and then plopped down in my chair, folding my arms over my chest. He continued, "We have three safe houses in which we will sleep tonight. The buses will take us to the airport at five in the morning."

"What about Mom and Amy? And the rest of my stuff?" I asked.

"They'll meet us at the airport and the rest of our stuff will be packed for us."

"I'll pack an extra suitcase for you, Ronni," Jenny offered as her lower lip trembled. "I have nothing to pack."

"Thanks," I said feeling guilty.

"The people who stay behind will make sure the rest of our stuff gets to us."

"Mom is going to freak out about her paintings and Persian carpets."

"Your mom's stuff will be packed up with care like everything else," Dad said.

"We can't say goodbye," I said. I would never see Ellen, Ian, the O'Malleys, or anyone ever again. I didn't know anyone in Maryland.

"We'll see everyone on the plane," Dad said.

"I need to call Ellen, Ian, Rocky, and Nancy."

"The phone is only for emergencies." *Checking on my friends was an emergency.*

"I feel sick. Can I be excused?" I complained, "I don't want any pumpkin pie."

"Yes, go pack a suitcase for your sister."

At least in Morocco we had a week to say goodbye, to cry and promise to write, to exchange addresses. I had to get a hold of Ellen. I had to know if she was all right.

Where would I begin packing up my life again? I flipped through my diaries full of memories starting from when I turned seven—should I pack them? What about the scrapbooks with every letter I ever received? I took out the most recent letter from Frana.

It read, "My Dearest Ronni, Sometime when I get really sad, I remember you. Yesterday someone spat at me as I crossed the street. He called me a rag-headed Iranian. The United States will never be my home, but I can never go back to Iran either." Poor Frana. I was fortunate; I could go home, but where was that?

I knew I should thank my lucky stars to have things to pack, but I didn't want to leave any of them behind. I stuffed my diaries and letters into my suitcase. Mom would have said suitcases are for clothes but I had different priorities. I would have packed Ellen and Ian and all my other friends if I could. *Where was Rocky? Would I ever see Ellen again? Or hear Ian tell a stupid joke?*

At seven o'clock, someone rapped at my door. "What do you want?" I snarled expecting my dad to buzz around and see how much I'd packed.

Rashid entered and closed the door behind him. "You want see your friend?" he whispered.

"Yes, but I don't know where she is."

"You come," he said. He held out a chador, a black habit-like costume a nun might wear. "You wear this. We go embassy."

I smiled at him. "The embassy burned down, Rashid. Thanks but no one's there."

He tugged at my arm. "Yes, we go find your friend."

"Thanks, Rashid, but Ellen's house burned down. She's gone."

He ignored me and walked to the door. "We walk, no rupees."

I couldn't walk especially with rioter and military guards on every street corner. "It's no use, Rashid. It's dangerous. Ellen isn't there anymore."

He turned and pushed the chador in my hands. "We find, Runny."

I glanced back at my jewelry box. It was open and on top was my 24-karate blue sapphire and diamond ring. I bought it in Hong Kong for a steal, sixty dollars. I thought it was the nicest thing I'd ever own. I picked it up. "Could we trade this for a ride to find her?"

He studied my face before taking the ring. "I go. You wait. I call you." He scurried away.

Twenty minutes later, I heard a whistle out my window. Rashid stood under the tree. I scampered down. He helped me into the chador and we ran to the street corner. At the curb sat a silver Pontiac Bonneville. Rashid hustled me into the car. I froze.

Muhammed sat in the driver's seat, his hands clutching the wheel. His eyes stared at me in the rear view mirror.

Oh shoot! He hated me. He'd kicked me out of his house because of Jimmy Carter. But he'd let me go at the school. Was he taking me hostage? Was Rashid working with him? If he kidnapped me no one would know where I was. I grasped the door handle. I had to escape. Rashid seized my hand. He and Muhammed started yelling at one another. Muhammed gestured at me a dozen times.

"I'll get out." I tried the door again. "We can walk, Rashid. I don't want to cause any problems." *Or end up dead.*

"No, Runny. Okay," Rashid said.

Muhammed continued to glare at me through the mirror. "You greedy Americans try to buy your way through everything." He hardly had any accent. What was he talking about? I didn't think I could buy my way out of things. I didn't mean to insult him with the ring.

"If you hate me so much, why didn't you attack us at the school?" I asked.

"I don't beat up women and children. But you Americans and your Jimmy Carter, you damaged our great mosque in Mecca. You don't care about anything."

I remembered how Frana had been treated and felt sad. Every culture had its own villains. "The Marine who got shot, he didn't do anything to your mosque," I argued.

"You don't respect our laws or customs," Muhammed said.

"I'm sorry," I said, remembering the first day I got to Pakistan and how I'd looked down on the natives.

"What?" Muhammed spun around to stare me in the eye.

"I'm sorry your mosque was ruined." I flinched under his scrutiny. "No one should attack a place of worship."

Muhammed grunted. After a minute he pulled my ring out of his shirt pocket and handed it to me. "I don't need your ring." I took it. *So, blackmail wasn't his plan.*

The car accelerated and Rashid put a blanket over my head. I hunkered beneath it as we zigzagged our way through the town. Suddenly, Muhammed stopped the car. "You get out here," he said.

Where were we? I pulled the blanket off my head. Squinting through the darkness, I recognized the street before the embassy, and over the buildings an orange glow of fire and black smoke. A shiver of fear ran down my spine. "Thanks," I said. "Rashid, you coming?"

"No, we be back. You find friend." The car took off as I worried about what to do if Ellen wasn't there. What if I got lost? How would I find the car again?

Flames lashed out from where the embassy once stood and ash floated down on me. The mangled iron gate was covered in barbed wire. A pile of rubble stood where a brick wall once was. At least a dozen armed Marines in camouflage uniforms stood guard around the perimeter. By the ash pile was a solitary figure. I knew it was Ellen long before I was close enough to identify her.

"Step back. You can't be—" A Marine startled me by suddenly materializing before me. He held a gun. I'd never seen him before.

"Wait, I'm an embassy dependent. Don't shoot. I'm taking this off." I pointed to the chador and put my hands up to show him I wasn't armed. I inched the outfit over my head.

"Who are you and what do you want?" he asked lowering his rifle.

"My name is Ronni Wasp. Who are you? And where are our Marines?"

"We're back-up. They're here too."

"Where is Sergeant Ross? He'll let me in. I need to see my friend. She's standing over by the fire." I spotted Rocky coming towards us. "Rocky, let me in. It's Ronni."

He hustled over and the other Marine let me pass. "What are you doing out? It's not safe," Rocky asked.

"I had to come for Ellen." I ran to her. "God, I'm so sorry," I said, hugging her.

"Oh, Ronni." She clutched me.

"I know." I brushed a tear from the corner of her eye.

"I really loved him," she said. "We were going to get married. What am I going to do?"

"I don't know," I said.

"My mom and I are leaving for Delhi tomorrow with some of the other teachers."

"You're not going to the States with us? Why not? I'll never see you again, will I?" My eyes filled and I hugged her again.

"I don't know. We can write and when I get back to the States—" she stopped for a minute. "Ronni, I've lost everything. I'm going to miss him so much. How can I say goodbye?"

I shook my head. Goodbye should have been easy; we'd had so much practice, but every time it ripped at my heart. I gave her another hug. "I don't know." I sniffed back tears and I couldn't say anything to comfort her. And I'd probably never see her again. I heard the sound of distant gunshots. Ellen and I hit the ground. *Not again. We weren't safe anywhere.*

Rocky rushed over to us. His radio crackled and sputtered out a halted message, "Two teenagers missing. Search for the girls and get them to the safe house." Did that mean us? "I have to get you guys back," Rocky said. "The streets aren't safe. Ronni, I'm calling your dad. Ellen, yours is here."

I grabbed her hand and we held on to each other for a moment then Ellen broke away and left. She looked back one last time and I waved. "I'll always remember you," I yelled after her.

"Come on, Ronni. Your dad will be here any minute. Stay with me." Rocky took my arm.

I touched his shoulder. "Rocky, I'm sorry about Kevin."

He turned away for a moment before looking back. His eyes were red. For a moment, we stared at one another. We exchanged thoughts in those seconds that didn't require words. I knew he didn't want to cry in front of me. "I'm real sorry," I repeated.

His lips buckled over one another as he uttered, "I know."

And then I did it. I hugged him. My cheek brushed his cold, starched, camouflage jacket. He didn't move for a while. Then I felt his hand on my back and he hugged me back. After a moment he pulled back and said, "It's okay now."

I raised my head. "I'm glad I saw you guys before I have to leave," I said. He just nodded. I forced a smile. "I wanted to thank you for my dad," I added.

"He's welcome."

"Are you going to be okay?" I asked.

"I'm a Marine. I have to be. Come on, Ronni, you're going home. Take New York home with you." Then he placed a gloved hand over his forehead and a single tear escaped the corner of his eye while his lips trembled. Kevin's coffin was going with us to the States. Rocky let me know that he wanted me to watch out for his friend.

I turned to spare him. "I will. I promise," I whispered. I didn't know how I was going to get through another goodbye.

Chapter Twenty-Four

All the way home Dad lectured me. "You know you shouldn't be out on the streets. What were you thinking? I didn't know where you were." I sat next to him, staring out the window as he chewed me out the whole way home. Okay, I'd scared him but what choice did I have? He wouldn't let me use the phone.

As soon as he parked the Jeep, I jumped out and he called behind me, "Go get your suitcase. We're going to the Thorton's house."

Juma followed us to the door. "Come on, girl." I turned to my dad and asked, "Where's her cage?"

"We can't take her." *What—we weren't taking our dog? We always took her.*

"Huh?"

"She has to stay here. She'll be taken care of and sent along in a few days."

"By who? Who's going to feed her?" If it were up to our cook, Akbar, she would starve, being only a dirty beast.

"Ronni, don't start again. We can't take her. Let's go."

Our Juma Maguarde wagged her tail, confused, her eyes asking me to allow her to follow. "It's okay, girl. You stay here and guard the house. You'll see us on the other side." Dad loved her, too; he may have paid Akbar to take care of her. Muhammed's words came back to me, "You Americans think you can buy your way through anything."

There was one other person I had to say goodbye to, but Rashid was nowhere in sight. "Where's Rashid?" I asked my dad. He didn't answer; he clambered into the car.

I stood at the door and waited for Jenny Miller to drag little Susie out. Reluctantly, I petted Juma one last time. She jumped on me, whining to join in the adventure. The smart dog knew what suitcases meant. I held her back with my leg. She dug her neglected, long nails into my thigh.

"Ouch. No, girl. It's okay." I shoved her back and slammed the door on her high-pitched whine of mistrust.

Rashid came around the side of the house as I walked to the car. "Runny?" he called. He had a little bag in his hand. "Runny, I go with you. You need help. I go with you."

I eyed his tiny bag with all his belongings. "No, Rashid. I'm sorry. We can't take you," I said.

"I work you."

"Sorry, Rashid. No work." Poor little kid. He had worked for us when we needed him—now we abandoned him.

"In your country, no cleaning?" he asked.

"Yes, but it's different. You wouldn't like it." How could he understand child labor laws or minimum wage?

"I help you," he argued. His eyes pleaded with me. *How could I just leave him?*

"I wish you could go, but I don't have money to bring you with me."

"Then you go. I find rupees. I follow," he said.

"It's very expensive to live there." I thought of how he had showed up in Kabul and at the house and a part of me wished that he would find a way to follow me.

"I get rupees. You no worry, Runny. I come help you."

How could I explain that our family wouldn't have servants in the U.S.? We couldn't pay anyone fifty cents a week or even a day to work for us. He wanted to go so badly, and I couldn't hurt his feelings. I reached down and rummaged through my bag and my jewelry box, ignoring Dad's demands that I had to hurry. "Okay, Rashid, here." I held out my diamond and sapphire ring. "Maybe this will help you find your way."

He put it in his palm and I closed my hand around both. "Where you go, Runny. I find you."

"Bye, Rashid," I said. I shook his hand, walked to the car and squeezed in next to Susie. My lip trembled. *Would the little kid be okay?* I nodded my head. If anyone could find his way it was Rashid.

In the tin teahouse at the end of Nara Lane, I saw a few men ending a day of heavy manual labor, laughing and drinking sweet tea. I took it all in, my last sights of a country I'd called home.

Cars congested the street in front of Bob Thorton's house. Because we arrived so late, we had to carry our bags two blocks. The heavy suitcases pulled our shoulders out of their sockets.

The entranceway was bright and so was Mr. Miller. "Are we late? Did we miss the party?" Mr. Thorton loomed over us and his black hair shadowed his face. He stuck out his big hand for the parents to shake.

"No. Come in, come in."

Orderly lines of suitcases lined the wall, and we quickly relieved ourselves of ours. It reminded me of the last time I went on a class trip to see the snow almost a year before in January.

"Everyone lay down on a bag or blanket. Lights out! Go to sleep!" Mr. Thorton ordered us. He snapped off the lights leaving us to grope our way in the dark.

As I walked towards the rear of the house, my foot struck someone on the floor, "Ouch!" the victim yelled.

"Oh sorry," I apologized to my unseen victim.

"Watch it," warned another victim.

"Sorry, I can't see in here." I stumbled and dodged over lumps on the floor.

"Ronni?" Ian's voice called through the darkness. "Over here!"

"Hey," I said, kneeling down.

"Ouch, watch it would ya!" someone said next to me.

"Sorry, man." I frowned down at the dark floor. It wasn't my fault I couldn't see. "Isn't there any space?"

"I saved you a spot here. Move over, Edward," Ian ordered his brother.

I sat down and my eyes adjusted to the dark.

"Hey, remember last time we had a co-ed sleepover?" he asked.

"Yeah, up in the hills at the Ambassador's vacation house. With all the snow."

"Yeah. I put my sleeping bag next to yours and you moved."

"I did not," I said. At the time I had thought Ian's bag next to mine was coincidental.

"Yes you did. That crushed me." I'm glad he couldn't see me blush in the dark.

"Would you two please be quiet!" someone on the floor called out.

I ignored them. "Sure Ian," I said. "You were dating Jackie."

"Yeah, but I wanted to go out with you."

"Shut up." I punched him lightly on the shoulder.

"Why don't you both shut up?" came from the darkness.

"God, that was ru . . . de," I said. I tried to lay down to sleep but guilt, sadness, and fear kept me awake. Finally, I rolled over to face Ian. I saw a silhouette of his face in the dark. "Ian, I wanted Ellen to break up with Kevin. I secretly hoped they'd break up."

"Why?" He propped himself up on his elbows so that moonlight from a crack in a curtain hit the lower half of his face.

"I guess—." Would he think I was an idiot if I told him? It was too late I'd already started, "—I was afraid. I didn't want to lose her friendship. And now he's dead. I just wish I had been happy for her. I didn't want things to change."

He softly brushed a strand of hair from in front of my face. "Ronni, you didn't kill him. He was shot. You don't have to feel guilty. Besides you'll never be alone. Any guy would love to be with you. You're beautiful."

"Oh, Ian, you're so stupid." I wiped at tears leaking down my cheeks. "But, thanks anyway." I laid down my head and closed my hot, overworked, wet eyes.

"Ronni?" Ian's voice sounded miles away.

"Yeah?" I didn't open my eyes.

"I'm going to Maryland when I get back. College Park. Isn't that where you're from?"

"Yeah. But our house is being rented. I don't know where we'll live. Why?"

"Well, we'd be going to school at the same high school. Maybe you could show me around," he said.

"You're going to North Western?" I opened my eyes and stared at him.

"Yeah." A glint of moonlight reflecting off white teeth made his smile look brilliant in his shadowy face.

"Maybe we could show each other around. I could always use a friend," I said, happy that I wasn't losing yet another person.

I closed my eyes to sleep but Ian said, "Ronni, I just wanted to tell you. I just wanted to say . . ."

"What?"

"Nothing. Goodnight.

*   *   *

Something buzzed in the distance. A voice shouted, "Okay everyone up! Time to go!"

"No." My head swam. *Where was I anyway?* I turned away from the annoying light that tried to knife its way under my eyelids. "Go away." I rolled over. Something hard stopped me.

A rough hand shook me and someone said, "Get up! Bus is here! Grab your stuff and let's go!"

I stood and picked up my blanket to fold but my knees buckled and my head spun as the strong odor of smoke that lingered on the men who had been trapped in the burning embassy filled the house. I dropped the blanket. The door opened, the cold morning air seeped in. I heard barks and whines. On the lawn were a dozen or more metal carriers containing excited pets.

"I guess the animals drove themselves over during the night," Mr. Thorton said.

Juma's cage rested among the others. The sight of the cage reminded me that I had promised to make sure Kevin's coffin got on the plane.

Chapter Twenty-Five

That morning, groups of soldiers massed on every street corner. In the gray dusk, the airport looked like a military headquarters. Instead of feeling safe, I felt like a prisoner—as though their guns pointed at me.

Mr. Thorton announced that we had had a two-hour delay until nine, when the plane was scheduled to take off. Besides our flight, P.I.A. number 74, there didn't appear to be other flights departing.

We spread ourselves throughout the entire waiting room. Some little ones slept; others ran around. Conversations started all around me.

"They found his body Thanksgiving Day. They say he died of smoke inhalation. His body was badly burnt."

Smoke inhalation. Kevin had been shot. That meant someone else had died. "Who else died?" I whispered to Ian.

"Sergeant Elvis. He died in the compound. He burned."

Wait, I knew him. I'd babysat for his three-year-old son and four-year-old daughter a few times. Were they with us in the waiting room? I peered around but didn't see them.

Mothers calmed little ones with crackers. I wanted something, something to make the nausea stop. The smell of smoke wouldn't quit. I wore the smell as though it penetrated my skin so deeply it scarred my soul. I popped my last piece of gum in my mouth.

I looked over my shoulder and spotted a man behind me sipping something out of a paper bag. He muttered, "I'll tell 'em the truth if they want it. The government would have let us burn in there. They come waltzing into the place when it's all over and we're supposed to thank them." He pretended to spit on the ground before continuing: "Well, President Carter can save his thanks to Zia. The big phony."

A man sitting next to him spoke, "You know it's not that simple. Zia had to be worried about the mob overthrowing his military."

"He'd have a lot more to worry about if we'd died. That is if anyone had had the balls to hold him responsible," the first man argued. They fell silent.

Across from me two women mopped tears from their cheeks. "Those poor men and their families."

"Only nineteen, can you imagine?" They were talking about Kevin. But he was only an idea to them. They only knew his age, not that he loved Ellen or how he loved to play cards and how intelligent he was.

"We're carrying the bodies back with us on the flight." Kevin and Sergeant Elvis were no longer people, they were luggage to be buried and forgotten.

I looked around the room. In a year, would all the people in the room be just as forgotten to me? I felt tired and my head hurt too much to think. I turned to Ian. "Can I use your shoulder?"

"Anytime." I leaned on him and his arm went around my shoulders. "Hey, is that peppermint? You got any more gum?"

"Last piece." I smiled up at him.

"Give me half."

"It's A.B.C. gum."

"So give me half." He grinned down at me and slid his hand behind my head. His lips touched mine. His tongue rubbed against my teeth as I opened my mouth to let him have the gum. I tasted the smoke from a cigarette on his tongue. I feared nicking his tongue if I tried splitting the gum. My first French kiss.

When he pulled away, I looked tentatively around the room. Did anyone see? What did it mean? I didn't know. We were friends. I searched his eyes for answers as he popped the gum from his mouth, bit it in two pieces and put half in my mouth.

I gave up trying to think it through, leaned my head against his shoulder, and dozed.

An hour later, we boarded P.I.A. # 74. Mom and Amy and others from the field trip were already on board. They had saved us two seats.

"Did you pack all my stuff?" Amy asked.

"We could only pack one suitcase each. Oh, and Susie Miller packed an extra bag for you. The rest of your stuff—I sold," I teased.

She laughed. "Where's my money?"

"The junk only went for fifty cents. I kept that for my commission. No." I laughed. "Just kidding. The shippers will be packing it. What was it like where you were?"

"We didn't hear anything until Thanksgiving and then they wouldn't let us go to Moenjordaro. We stayed in Lahore for Thanksgiving and had to act like the natives and put scarves over our heads. We borrowed long skirts and shirts to walk to the bus."

"Students came to the school too," I told her. "We thought they were going to attack us. Rashid's brother was there."

"Well we're glad you guys got out of your sticky situations," Mom said putting an arm around me. I kissed her cheek. Then I peered over Amy and out the window.

Would it be my last view of Pakistan? How could a place feel like home while still not feeling entirely safe? Until we took off, I wondered if we could be attacked at any time. In the air, I wondered if I'd ever feel so comfortable any place or if I'd ever be part of a community that understood how it felt to constantly start over?

Epilogue

At Dulles Airport, on the outskirts of D.C., we entered a waiting room packed with people. Some we knew from Islamabad, and others wanted a story.

Ian approached me. "I've got to leave. See you in school. Don't be a stranger." I hugged him.

His arms pulled me tightly to him. Over his shoulder, I saw Frana. "Ronni," she yelled, waving a dozen yellow roses. I broke away from Ian, kissed his cheek, ran to her, and hugged her. She was there. She'd come. Finally, I had my friend back. When we broke apart, she handed me the roses.

"Thanks. I'm so glad you're here," I said hugging her again.

We stood back and looked at each other a moment. Her bright yellow shirt made her skin glow a beautiful tan over new Levis and her black hair was shiny in its neat braid. "How are you?" she asked.

"Good. You look great," I said.

"Thanks, you look tired and you smell like smoke."

"Yeah."

"Where's your friend, Ellen?"

"She went to India with her family. But I have something I promised to do for her. Come on."

Mom and the rest of the family talked with a group of friends and I knew I wouldn't be missed.

"This way." I pulled her along by the hand.

I looked for signs that said baggage or cargo and finally I got to an information desk. "Excuse me," I asked. "Where would a coffin go off the last flight?"

"Ah . . . what?" the perplexed woman behind the counter asked in a southern accent.

"You know a coffin with a body? Where would it go?"

"You're not from the mortuary service, are you?" She crossing her arms over her chest and narrowed her eyes at us.

I hesitated. "What if we were?" I asked.

"What do you kids want?"

"We want to know where our friend is. We want to take him these flowers. We're off the Pan Am flight that just arrived from Frankfurt."

"Even if it I told you, you aren't allowed down there."

"I just want to know where it is."

"Right below us, down the stairs. In the cargo area." She looked around warily. "Don't try anything stupid," she warned, "Security's tight with those hostages in Iran."

"We won't," I assured her but I wasn't sure I wouldn't. "Thank you for your time."

I led Frana from the counter and went for the steps. Police officers stood everywhere. The place buzzed with excitement. I rubbed my hands together and tried to think of a way past them.

"Ronni, what are you thinking? I'm from Iran, remember? Are you crazy? Let's go back. It's a bad idea, enough already."

A police officer put out his hand as we tried to enter the stairwell. "What can I do for you ladies?"

I swallowed hard, trying to decide what to say. Then I spoke rapidly, "Good morning officer, we just got off Pan Am, from Frankfurt. We were evacuated. We're all greeting each other and rejoicing, but there are two that aren't up there. They're downstairs . . . ," my voice faltered but I quickly regained my composure. "They're in boxes draped with American flags. I have flowers to welcome them home."

"Whoa, what now?"

"There is a dead Marine and a dead Army Sergeant in the cargo area and we'd like to say goodbye to them." I rambled.

"You can't go down there. You'll have to wait for the memorial services."

"Then, can you welcome them home for us?" I held out the bouquet.

"What?"

"Could you lay the flowers on their coffins? So, the first thing their loved ones see are the roses. Don't yellow roses mean 'always loyal', Semper Fi?"

I saw something flicker in his eyes. Maybe it was only the reflection of water in my own, or maybe it was the ghost of a friend whose death he was remembering. "Wait, I'm an ex-Marine." He smiled, but didn't take the flowers. "Maybe I'm crazy. Come with me."

When we reached the basement area, we found a security guard in front of swinging double door. "What are those kids doing down here?" He questioned the police officer.

"Come to see the coffins."

"They can't do that," the guard grumbled, "and ain't that one from 'eye ran'?"

They both studied Frana. She gave me her 'I told you so' glare.

"Yes, she is from Iran," I admitted.

"Can't let anyone in there without proper documentation," the guard said.

"Not everyone from Iran is our enemy. Frana can't go home again because her dad worked for the Shah and they'd kill him."

"Compromise." The cop said. "Let the American in and security wand her."

"I want Frana to come with me," I pleaded. It was the least I could do. "Please, she was there, too. She knew Sergeant Elvis. She wants to say goodbye."

The men looked at me hard. I guessed I blew it. The ex-Marine would escort us up the stairs again for sure. I couldn't stand the silence. "Okay, I'm sorry I argued with you," I blurted out. "Just give them these and say goodbye." I held out the flowers again.

The cop took them, inspected them, and then ran a wand over the two of us. He opened the double doors. I saw two coffins, flanked by three military guards standing at attention.

The soldiers stared at the door. The cop put his finger to his lips and shook his head. "It's okay. We need just a minute."

I began to shake, thinking about those cops and guards watching us. Gray metal, gray and blue uniforms, and a tomb-like silence surrounded us. I looked at the flag-draped coffins. I didn't know which was Kevin's and which was Sergeant Elvis's, so I placed six roses on each flag. Then, I stood back and bowed my head.

"Ellen couldn't be here, Kev. I promised her I would instead. And Rocky, well, he . . . He's okay. He misses you. He . . . He's real proud of you, though. You'd have been proud of him too. You know he wouldn't leave you there alone. My dad told me he helped everyone out and then he came back for you. I'm so sorry." I quickly swiped at my eyes. "Anyway, we all miss you . . . But you already know that. I want you to watch over Rocky and Ellen, okay?"

My stupid eyes dripped again, damn them. I sniffed and turned towards the other coffin, even though I didn't know who was who. "Mr. Elvis, goodbye, watch over your kids. We'll always remember you guys."

I took Frana's hand and we climbed the stairs to a world full of life and laughter. I kept my promise, I never forgot about Pakistan, Rashid, Ellen, Kevin, Rocky, or anyone who shared that world with me.

MSG Classroon Named After Fallen Marine

MARINE CORPS BASE QUANTICO VA (Nov 30, 2006)

On November 21, staff and students from Marine Security Guard Battalion gathered in Classroom One of the MSG School for a ceremony to dedicate and rename the room after a fallen comrade. The day of the dedication marked the 27th anniversary of Cpl. Steven Crowley's death in the line of duty.

"On this day, twenty-seven years ago, Cpl. Crowley took his post not knowing what would take place." Said Col. David Head, MSG Bn. Commanding Officer, at the dedication ceremony. "All he knew was that he had a job to do and he was going to do that job."

On that fateful day in 1979, the American Embassy in Islamabad, Pakistan—where Crowley was stationed—came under the attack of hundreds of angry Pakistanis.

Submitted by: MCB Quantico
Story excerpt by: Lance Cpl. Travis J. Crewdson
Story Identification: 2006121143129